Marked and Mated

Delta James

Published by Stormy Night Publications and Design, LLC.
www.StormyNightPublications.com

Cover design by Korey Mae Johnson
www.koreymaejohnson.com

Images by The Killion Group, Shutterstock/thonephoto, and Dreamstime/Kaz Yamazaki

1st Print Edition. August 2018

ISBN-13: 978-1725173156

ISBN-10: 1725173158

FOR AUDIENCES 18+ ONLY

This book is intended for adults only. Spanking and other sexual activities represented in this book are fantasies only, intended for adults.

CHAPTER ONE

Jean-Michel Gautier, alpha of New Orleans, stood at the back of the room and listened as the fate of the all-female pack located on the Outer Banks of North Carolina was debated. He shook his head. Someone needed to drag these relics of another time into something even close to the twenty-first century.

The all-female pack known as Bae Diogel or Safe Harbor had successfully fought off a raid by a rogue band of Serbian wolves looking to capture the women and return to their homeland with them as mates. Things hadn't worked out so well for the Serbs. Not only had they been entirely unsuccessful, rumor had it that the women had killed several of them and had sent the rest home with their tails between their legs.

What an extraordinary group of women. How were they living, and it sounded like thriving, under the very noses of the Ruling Council without being detected? Jean-Michel thought to himself as the smile on his face grew wider. *What glorious mates they would be.*

Jean-Michel was a shifter-born as opposed to a human-turned. He could trace his wolf ancestry back hundreds of years. They say the last Gautier who had not been born a shifter was Jean Lafitte, the famous pirate from the late eighteenth/early nineteenth century. Much controversy and speculation still surrounded Lafitte's origins and death. Being a direct descendant, Jean-Michel knew that both had been obscured to cover up Lafitte's amazing ability to recover from what should have been mortal wounds and his longer than average life.

Gautier was the last surname that Lafitte had used before dying in his bed an old man surrounded by his mate and their offspring in the Crescent City… New Orleans. There had been a Gautier as the alpha of the New Orleans pack ever since that time. Jean-Michel had not only earned his place as alpha by means of heredity and alpha status but by being unanimously chosen by his pack to lead them.

Like most alpha males, Jean-Michel possessed an intimidating physical presence. He was a bit over six feet tall and had the muscular physique common to alphas. His hair was long and golden brown with dark streaks running through it. He had a well-developed core with chiseled abs and well-defined arms and legs. He had a sensual mouth and laughing eyes.

The New Orleans pack was one of the oldest, wealthiest, and most stable in the world and had been for centuries. Treasure inherited from Lafitte himself and invested wisely had ensured the pack would never be without a home or the funds it needed to sustain itself.

Jean-Michel was known to be generous to a fault and quick to laugh, but those who had done so, knew it was dangerous to cross him. His pack had wanted to see him mated for some time. He preferred to enjoy the company of many females—both wolf and human—until he heard the call of his true mate. The story passed down from generation to generation in his family was that the male members of his family would always know their fated mate by the faint fragrance of crepe jasmine that was an integral part of her distinctive scent.

Jean-Michel barely paid attention to the debate on the floor of the Council's meeting place. There were some pack leaders, a small minority, who felt, as he did, the way to resolve the problem of Bae Diogel was to invite them into the Council and then work toward integrating them into one or more of the established packs. At the same time, they could be offered the protection of the Council—although they may not see a need for it. Unfortunately, the majority of his brethren seemed to believe they could dictate to the rogue band of females that they disband and agree to be mated to an alpha of the Council's choosing.

Jean-Michel agreed that they should be integrated into established packs but not forcibly. He also believed that trying to dictate anything to these women who had carved out a life and a place for themselves would not be accomplished easily or peacefully. Could the Council not see that the women of Bae Diogel would fight and kill to protect themselves and their home? He began to consider options for ensuring one or more of them came to find New Orleans as home. His pack, at this point, was overrun with unmated males, himself among them. Could the one he'd been waiting for be in North Carolina? Was that where she'd been hiding?

He turned from his musing back to the matter at hand. It had come to a vote. As he had thought it would, the majority voted to issue Bae Diogel an invitation, basically a demand, to disband and surrender themselves to the Council for their futures to be decided. Jean-Michel's fears about how badly this might go were mitigated somewhat when he heard Dylan Grainger, one of those who voted against the proposal, was to head up the retrieval and reintegration of the women.

Jean-Michel walked out of the Council's chambers shaking his head and laughing at the foolishness of those who believed they could honor the past by refusing to look to and embrace the future.

•••••••

Darby Callan sat and listened as Skylar Owen, alpha of Bae Diogel, outlined their choices… none of which was good. They had successfully defended themselves and their home when a pack of wolves from Serbia had crossed the Atlantic and attacked. Even though they were surprised by the actual attack, they had always anticipated someone trying to curtail their freedom.

Darby had come to Bae Diogel after having left an abusive mate. The very thought of having to be in his presence again made her shudder. The man who had turned her mother and then sired Darby had given her to the alpha of a rival pack in settlement of a debt. He had marked her as his mate and then abused her. Finally, one night when he had passed out drunk while still inside her, Darby had managed to push him off and escape. The rumors of an all-female pack off the coast of North Carolina had been whispered among the females of the wolf-shifter society for years. They were said to offer a safe harbor to female wolves in need. Taking only the clothes on her back, she had fled into the night.

Darby had been with the women of Bae Diogel for almost two years. It was the first place she'd ever felt was her home. When they were attacked by the Serbian wolf pack, they had all fought viciously to send them packing and to stay together. Both Skylar and Roz, the alpha and beta respectively of their pack, had cautioned them not to celebrate too quickly. They both feared that the attack and their success in fighting it off would probably bring unwanted attention to their existence. There was grave concern that the Ruling Council would take the notion of an all-female pack as an affront and move against them. That concern had come home to roost this morning when a messenger had delivered an ultimatum from the Ruling Council.

"But, Sky, we sent those Serbs packing… at least the ones we sent home…"

"I know. But that was one small pack. And they weren't

anticipating much, if any, of a defense on our part. If the Ruling Council moves against us, it'll be all of the packs in the US and Canada. We don't stand a chance against them."

"Then what are you suggesting we do?"

"Anyone who wants to stay is welcome to do so with my blessing. But I won't stay and I can't win if I fight, so I'm going to run. If we move quickly we may be able to outmaneuver them."

"What do you mean by quickly?"

"This afternoon. Anyone wanting to come, gather your things and meet me on the dock. Does anyone want to stay?" Skylar searched each of the seven faces she had come to call pack and family. She smiled sadly. "I didn't think so. Then once we're outside, I'm going to torch our home."

There was a collective gasp and murmurs not to do it.

Sky held up her hand. "No, there's too much of us here. Too many things they might be able to use against us. And if I'm going to be forced from my home, I'll be damned if I leave them anything but ashes. Now, let's get moving. Their noose may be already closing around us."

The women dispersed and grabbed those possessions they held most dear. They were assembled outside within the hour. Skylar had started a fire in the fire pit on the patio. There were eight torches. Each woman took a torch and went to a designated spot next to the house. Together and as one they set fire to their past and all their hopes for the future. Skylar watched as each of them fought back her tears and headed for the Zodiac on the dock.

Anna joined Skylar and Roz and handed Skylar a small electronic device. "That ought to do the trick," she said. "You should be able to control the sailboat and sail it right into the bastards if they're out there. Oh, Sky, I'm so…"

"Don't, Anna. We can't afford to indulge our worries and sorrows. We need to forge ahead. If we're to pull this off, we're going to need all of us operating at maximum strength and capacity."

They joined the other women. Skylar turned the device

on and found that Anna had outdone herself. The sailboat handled almost as if she were aboard. Anna had installed a failsafe switch, and once thrown, there was no going back. The sailboat's engines would come to life at full throttle and a small incendiary device would send it up in flames.

Skylar maneuvered the sailboat out in front of the Zodiac. Roz sat at the bow opposite her, and Darby had the tiller of the Zodiac and piloted it behind the sailboat at a safe distance.

One of the cabin cruisers they'd seen patrolling the water off their island was closing fast. The big cabin cruiser stopped squarely in the middle of the channel between two sand spits ostensibly blocking their way. As the Zodiac could easily pass him on either side, the man in charge of the cabin cruiser was proving himself a fool. A powerful male voice came over a PA system: "Women of Bae Diogel. Stop and prepare to be boarded."

"Who the hell does he think he is, the British Navy?" asked Roz.

Skylar smiled at her. "I don't much care. If he doesn't move his ass fast enough, he'll be abandoning his own boat and hopefully his buddies in the other boat will go save them."

The disembodied voice repeated its command as the sailboat came closer and the Zodiac powered down. Skylar motioned to Darby to ease back on the throttle of the Zodiac. They needed to put distance between it and the sailboat. When the latter was about twenty-five yards from its target, Skylar hit the failsafe switch. As Anna had intended, the sailboat's engines engaged at full throttle making a beeline for the heavy cabin cruiser. A few seconds later, the whole thing went up in flames. A moment after that, it crashed broadside into the cabin cruiser, forcing her crew to jump into the ocean.

Darby gunned the engine on the Zodiac and sped around the flaming boats and crew. She made for open water as fast as the Zodiac would go.

Darby heard Roz shout to Skylar over the cheers of their pack, the curses of the men in the water, and the roar of the fire. "The other cabin cruiser looks like it's headed to save their buddies. I think we've made it."

"Not bloody likely," called Skylar. "The man they put in charge is ex-Special Forces; if he's sent that cabin cruiser to help those men, he's not far from here and means to catch us himself." Skylar took over the Zodiac's engine and tiller from Darby.

Darby moved up to the bow opposite Roz. They both watched as Lacey, the pack's omega, tried to encourage everyone to not lose heart. Skylar maneuvered the Zodiac close to the shore into more shallow water, hoping that whatever Dylan Grainger had coming after them would draw too much water to get close.

Darby was the first to see the power boat closing on them. "Sky, look, they've spotted us." Skylar increased the power to the Zodiac's engine trying to put as much distance between them as possible. "Shit!" called Darby. "The boat's a smuggler's boat. They're going to be able to follow us into shallow water."

Once again, they were hailed with a PA system. "Enough, Skylar. You can't get away. I've got more power and speed than you. Heave to and let's conclude this peacefully."

The women of Bae Diogel responded as one with a one-fingered salute from every member of her pack on the Zodiac with her.

Again, the PA crackled. "Naughty. Naughty. That's a very disrespectful way to respond to a courteous request. Let's try again. Heave to or we'll run you aground. I've got men trained to engage the enemy with me and you won't get far. Any woman who has to be chased down will get her bottom spanked hard enough that she'll need to stand for the ride back to Calon Gwyllt. But heave to and we'll forget this bit of nonsense ever happened."

Skylar, recognizable even at a distance by her wild mane

of red hair, handed the rudder over to one of her pack, stood up in the Zodiac, turned, leveled a flare gun at him and fired. He only had a minute to push more power to his engines and steer away, barely avoiding being hit with the flare.

Skylar took control of the Zodiac and called to the women she had vowed to protect, "This is it. I'm going onto the beach at full speed. Leave your things, shift, and run for your lives. I'll try to hold them back if I can."

"We won't leave you, Sky."

"You have to. Don't you see? If even one of us gets away, she can live her life for the rest of us. Promise me. All of you."

They nodded as Skylar gunned the engines once again and headed straight for the beach.

The Zodiac hit the beach at full speed, creating a furrow of one hundred yards before its engine gave out. The women jumped out, shifted into their wolf forms, and ran scattering along the beach. The speedboat came in right behind them but stopped just short of running aground.

Dylan's men hit the beach, shifting as they did so and each headed after the woman he had been assigned to capture. They gave Skylar a wide berth.

•••••••

Darby heard Dylan shout to one of his men, "Get after her, Matthew. She's taken off to the hard right!"

Darby shifted into her wolf form and ran for all she was worth. The blood pumped through her veins as she tried to outrun the wolf she could hear behind her. One by one, the men who served the man the Council had sent to destroy them ran down her pack mates. Only she and Roz remained free. But then Roz was taken down by a large gray wolf with a white-tipped tail. He grabbed her by the scruff of the neck and shook her until she relented and reverted to human form.

Darby could hear the breathing of the large wolf closing the distance between them. She'd almost made the dunes when he pounced, knocking the wind out of her. He too grabbed her by the scruff of her neck and shook. Darby growled, snarled, and tried to reach back to bite him. It did no good. He was bigger, stronger, and had her pinned. Reluctantly she too shifted back.

"It's all right. No one wants to hurt you," said the man Grainger had called Matthew, who now had hold of her arms to keep her from bolting.

"No, of course not. I heard your leader, he means to see all of us beaten for not doing as we're told."

Matthew chuckled. "Why is it that whenever one of you girls gets caught doing something naughty and is held accountable, we get accused of beating you?"

"What would you call it?"

"I would call it well-deserved punishment for your misbehavior this afternoon. Nice stunt with the sailboat by the way. Dylan was impressed."

"I don't give a damn about impressing whoever this Dylan bastard is."

"You'd best learn to give a damn. He's your new alpha. I'm sure he'll make certain allowances given your circumstances, but he won't tolerate disrespect. Best you keep a civil tongue in your head." Matthew stood and brought her up with him. "What's your name?"

Darby stared at him and said nothing. Matthew shook his head and led her back to the beach to join the other members of Bae Diogel. As they were approaching, Darby heard Skylar call to Roz.

"How many, Roz?"

"All of us, Sky. They have us all." Roz sounded as defeated as she'd ever heard her; her voice indicated she was on the verge of tears. Roz never cried. Darby searched those on the beach. None of them had escaped. Seeing that Roz was correct was like a physical blow.

Dylan offered Skylar a deal. His voice was firm, but not

unkind.

"It'll be all right, Sky," he started. "I won't let that little maneuver with the flare gun or you threatening me with a knife go without punishment. And I hate to tell you, but I think that punishment needs to be now for your pack's sake, for my men's sake, and frankly for your sake. The sooner you recognize and accept my authority over you, the easier this will be on everyone. But I'll make you a deal."

"You have nothing to offer me that I want," answered Skylar.

"I think I do. I had planned to have your pack disciplined before we head for home. My thought was if the lot of you were nursing sore bottoms, you'd be a lot easier to deal with on a small boat. But, if you put down the knife and submit to my authority, you'll be the only one spanked. I'll give the others a pass as having acted on your orders. But mark my words, I intend to make your first spanking from me memorable."

"That's not much of a deal."

"Oh, but it is," he said with the barest hint of a smile on his face. "Either way, I intend to go sit down on that log, put you over my knee, bare your pretty little backside, and paddle it until it's bright red and swollen. Get nasty while I'm doing it, and you'll get your first taste of my belt. Take my deal and you're the only one who gets spanked. Refuse my deal, I'll disarm you, spank you until you're crying, and take my belt to your backside and leave welts behind. And your pack members will each get a good taste of the discipline they obviously need before we head for home. So, what is it to be, mate? Just you or your women too?"

Darby watched Skylar search Dylan's face for the veracity and severity of his words. There wasn't a woman among them who didn't realize he was willing to spare them, but only if Skylar submitted.

"I have your word they won't be disciplined for our bid for freedom?" Skylar asked softly.

"You do."

Skylar took the knife and threw it, landing it precisely between Dylan's spread feet.

The men all seemed surprised when Skylar surrendered, but the women who called her alpha were not surprised in the least. To the bitter end, Skylar would defend them as best she could.

The women were loaded on board the powerboat, unable to help their leader as the man who called himself her mate sat down on a log, bared her bottom, and then put her across his knee and began to spank her. All Darby could hear was the lapping of the water against the side of the boat and Dylan's hand connecting with Skylar's ass. She and the others struggled to no avail.

"It'll be all right," whispered Matthew. "The sooner she learns to yield to him, the easier it will be for her. He won't hurt her."

"Really? Ever had your ass beaten by someone big and brawny? Hot news flash, it's painful."

Matthew smiled and stroked her hair. "I know. But she's been naughty for some time and particularly so this afternoon. There's no way Dylan could let that slide. Some members of the Council already want his head on a platter for being so lenient with you ladies. Now settle down. She's his fated mate. He's been waiting for her. Hopefully, Dylan will be able to find yours as well."

"I won't mate again. You'll have to kill me."

Matthew chuckled. "Don't be so melodramatic. No one is going to kill you. In fact, there are some that will like that defiant, sassy attitude. I'm not one of them so if you keep poking at me, I'll ask Dylan to make an exception for you not getting spanked and see to it myself. Now sit down while you can still do so comfortably."

Finally, the sound of Skylar being punished ceased and she was allowed to get on the boat with the tall man the pack at Calon Gwyllt called alpha. He kept Skylar from joining her women and kept her at his side. The trip back to Calon Gwyllt was long and would have been cold save for the blanket Matthew insisted on wrapping around her.

CHAPTER TWO

When they arrived back at Calon Gwyllt, more men greeted them on the docks. Darby wasn't sure what they had expected, but apparently it wasn't angry and defiant women. When one of them tried to help her off the boat, Darby snatched her hand away from him and growled deep in her throat.

"That's enough," said the man on the dock. "I'm Nick. I am beta of Calon Gwyllt. You growl again and you won't make it to your room before you get your bottom bared and get a taste of the discipline you need."

Dylan spoke with the ranking members of his pack and had the women dispersed to various residences on the large estate. Darby was going to the same house as Anna. Anna flashed her a quick grin. Darby didn't react. She didn't know what Anna had up her sleeve, but then neither did the male wolves that surrounded them.

Both Anna and Darby were shown to a lovely set of rooms that were not adjacent to each other. Simon, the house leader tried to be cordial but Darby was terrified. She had learned in the past two years to take her fear and turn it to anger. That anger could fuel whatever she needed to get through a difficult situation. She had no doubt the Ruling

Council would send her back to her abusive mate. She wouldn't go. She would literally rather be dead.

As they were separated at the top of the stairs, Anna made the comment that it was too bad they didn't have a sailboat. The male wolves looked at her with curiosity and Darby was led to her room wondering what the hell she'd meant by that.

One of the women of the house was prattling on about clothes and dinner and showing her that her room had its own en suite bath.

"Get out," said Darby.

"I can stay if you like. We're all so glad you're here."

"And I, for one, would rather be dead than to be here."

"Oh, goodness. That's not good. No one will hurt you here."

"Really? Tell that to my alpha…"

"Someone hurt Dylan?" she asked, confused.

"That bastard is not my alpha. Skylar Owen of Bae Diogel is my alpha. Now get the hell out."

The woman started for the door and then stopped and turned. "I really am sorry you're so unhappy. If I can do anything, just ask Tim, he's right outside your door." She walked through it quickly. As the door closed behind her, Darby threw a vase filled with fresh flowers in her direction and watched it crash against the door.

Darby spent the next few hours checking the room to see if there was an obvious escape. There wasn't. Every time someone came through the door, Darby found something else to throw in their direction. When they tried to bring her something to eat, she shoved the door closed, forcing the tray back into the bearer and spilling its contents all over his clothes.

"Sailboat?" she said quietly. "Why would Anna want a sailboat?" And then it hit her and she had to suppress the urge to laugh. Anna was making a reference to technology. Anna had been their hacker and resident technology geek. Earlier when they had been forced to flee their home, Anna had rigged the sailboat so that Skylar could use it as a weapon. The sailboat had been empty and was driven by remote control. Skylar had merely pressed a button to get it to head full speed into a cabin cruiser blocking their way and burst into flames, forcing the men aboard the cabin cruiser to abandon their vessel by jumping into the water. Darby realized Anna must have found a way to hide something on her person that she thought might be able to help them get away.

There was a knock at the door and a very angry Nick entered. "What part of *that's enough* are you questioning?"

"The part where you have any authority to tell me that and expect me to comply."

"As of this afternoon, you and yours became members of this pack. That makes you and your misbehavior my concern and responsibility."

"What? Did the big bad boys of your pack tattle on me?"

"No, I met one of them coming downstairs with the food you managed to spill all over him. Everyone here is trying to make allowances for the loss we're sure you and yours are feeling. But I will not allow you to continue to behave like this. No one here wants to see any of you hurt."

"Did they not tell you that your fearless leader blackmailed my alpha into surrendering herself to his abuse?"

Nick laughed. "Is that the problem? Your former alpha disrespected and physically threatened the alpha of our pack. The fact that she is his mate does not make the offense any less. He provided the correction and discipline she needed and will get now that she's with him. And if you're not careful, you're going to find yourself in the same position over my knee for the very same reason."

Darby decided that fighting with Nick was not in her best interest and decided to try a different tactic. She began to cry softly. The tears weren't real, but the emotion behind them was. "I'm sorry, Beta. It's just been a very difficult day."

"I'm sure it has been. But you have to admit your behavior since you arrived has been nothing short of nasty."

"I think the tray of food was a bit over the top even for me," she said, smiling shyly.

"Just a bit? If you think that's just a bit over the top, I think you're going to spend the majority of your time here standing in the corner."

"Yes, Beta," she said, adopting a more submissive pose. "Would you mind apologizing to him for me until I see him again?"

"I can do that. Do you think you can behave more appropriately from now on?"

"I can try."

"I'm going to let you have this one pass. You will stay in your room and have supper up here. If your behavior improves, you can join the rest of the pack in the morning. But if I hear about one more tantrum, I will come back up here, bare that bottom, and give you a spanking you won't forget any time soon. Do you understand me?"

"Yes, Beta."

"All right. Darby?"

"Yes, Beta?"

"Don't make me regret this."

"Yes, Beta."

The door closed and in a childish display of temper she stuck out her tongue. She figured if he could treat her like a child, she could display the behavior of one.

•••••••

A few hours later, there was a knock on the door and a pretty blonde came through it bearing food and wine.

"I'm Bianca. You met my mate, Nick, earlier."

Darby nodded.

"You're lucky he was in a generous mood. Trust me when I tell you, that's not a knee you want to get put across. And those hands that can bring me such extreme pleasure are nasty when being applied to your backside for punishment."

"A lot of firsthand experience with that?" Darby asked, liking the blonde despite the circumstances of their meeting.

"Unfortunately, yes. Susannah thought she remembered your drink of choice was a good pinot noir. Mine too. This is one of my favorites. I also brought up something to eat. I understand that food brought to you earlier somehow got spilled."

Darby grinned. "Yes. Somehow it just flew up and spilled all over the guy. Must be gremlins."

Bianca laughed. "Yes, that must be it."

Darby spent an enjoyable hour talking with Bianca and enjoying an excellent bottle of pinot. She tried to find out as much about the estate and where it was situated as she could without tipping her hand. She could tell that Bianca was trying to get her to relax and accept what had happened. For now, until Anna revealed her plan, she would play nice.

Darby sat watching out the window as most of the residents of the house headed downstairs for dinner… including the guard at her door. Once the dinner party seemed to be in full swing, there was a quiet knock on the door and Anna let herself in.

"Okay, let's get some pillows put together so if they do a quick bed check, they'll think we're still here."

"But how?"

Anna grinned. "I managed to conceal a smart phone among the things that got delivered after we got here. I tapped into their security feed and recorded more than an hour. I've been working on the video to manipulate the changing shadows and lighting so that we can interrupt their live feed and load it on a continuous loop. That should give us the time we need to get the hell out of here."

"Do you think we can get to any of the others?"

"No, but once we're free we can put together a plan to come back and get them. Agreed?"

"You know it."

They waited until the guards passed under the window to Darby's room. Anna tapped into the estate's security system once again and downloaded the altered feed. Once they were sure it hadn't been detected, they slipped off the balcony and made a run for it.

The run across the open lawn was terrifying and exhilarating. When they reached the relative security of the heavily wooded area, they were almost giddy. Their plan appeared to be working. They stayed hidden and watched. Once the party at the main house had come to an end and the residents of the houses seemed to be settling down, Anna and Darby planned to make their next move. They would have to cover open ground and they needed both darkness and no wandering guards in order to be successful. They were about to proceed when they heard a cry from the residence in which they'd been placed. Their escape had been discovered.

"Shit!" whispered Darby. "We're going to need…" She stopped midsentence when they heard a young male wolf's mournful howl. Darby wasn't sure what it meant, until she saw Anna shudder. "Are you kidding me?"

"It's not my fault, Darby. I've done my best to avoid him. It feels like somebody just grabbed my lungs and squeezed. I can barely breathe."

"It's all right, Anna." The howl came on the wind and the effect it had on Anna was powerful. "He's your mate and he's calling for you. You need to decide if you want to stay or run. But, from the sound of it and the way your body is responding, he won't stop until he's found you."

"I don't know what I want. But you need to run and get away from me and from this place. I'll shift and see if I can't lead them away from you. Maybe with me as a distraction you can get to Roz or Skylar."

"No, the alpha here will have already planned for that. I'll try to get away, but let the others know I won't be far. I'll come back for you… all of you who want to go."

Darby watched as Anna shifted into her wolf form. She

had a rare true black coat, one that gave off an almost blue cast in the moonlight. The young male wolf called for her again. Anna shuddered in response but kept herself from returning the call. She looked over her shoulder at Darby, wagged her tail sadly, and sprinted away from her.

Deciding she could make better time as a wolf, Darby shifted as well. Her tawny brown coat with silver tips should let her be well hidden if she kept to the shadows of the trees. She moved through the woods quietly but as quickly as stealth would allow. She heard Anna's mate call to her again.

Once shifted, all of one's senses became more acute. Darby could see better in the dark, she could hear the group of shifted men approaching, and she could smell the ocean. As Anna had headed toward the ocean, Darby turned the other way. She hoped her friend could lead them away from her but knew that simply waiting was a fool's game.

Darby stopped and stilled the sound of her own heartbeat. They hadn't all gone after Anna, some of them had picked up her scent and were headed her way… fast. Stealth no longer served her needs. They would now be tracking her scent. Darby ran for where she thought the borders of Dylan's estate and the highway beyond might lay. Her only hope was to get to the road and shift back to human form when she heard a vehicle approaching.

Those who pursued her no longer worried about stealth either. They were close enough now that they began to bay in anticipation of catching her. Darby tried to increase her speed. They were gaining on her. She could see the wall that bordered the estate. There was no exit or gate readily available. She ran in the direction that led away from the ocean. She hated to be on open ground but there was no help for that. Darby darted out of the woods and ran for her life.

Her heart and lungs were operating at maximum capacity. She could hear the wolves behind her and saw something heading out of the woods on an intercept course. She tried to run faster and was in sight of the large gate, which was closed and being guarded. Darby was trying to formulate her next move when she was broadsided by a big gray wolf. They tumbled over the grass together. Before she could regain her feet, he had her pinned. Once again, she was grabbed by the scruff of her neck and shaken. She collapsed in defeat and resumed her human form.

Her captor shifted as well but continued to pin her to the ground as the others joined him. She heard him say, "Dylan? We have her. We have Darby. She never made it off the estate." He got off the phone and looked down at her. "Naughty wolf. I imagine Nick's going to blister your butt when we get back to the house."

One of the wolves that had pursued her was carrying clothes for her and tossed them to her. "You need to put those on. My mate suggested them, especially the pull-on pants. There's little doubt you're going to have your bottom bared in short order. If your behavior so far is any indication, that will happen to you frequently."

Darby stood and pulled on the clothes. She thought about refusing but decided it was a foolish and empty gesture. She didn't voluntarily go with them but offered little resistance when two wolves each took one of her arms and propelled her toward the house. Darby could see the rest of the women from Bae Diogel had been gathered together.

Anna was with one of the young wolves with whom they'd tangled this afternoon. He had his arm around her and seemed to be trying to comfort her. Darby was the last of the Bae Diogel pack to enter the house.

•••••••

Dylan addressed the assembled pack. "As some or most of you know, two of the ladies formerly of the Bae Diogel pack made a bid for their freedom this evening. They failed. Neither of them ever made it off the estate. While I'm sympathetic to the feeling these ladies may have about how their pack was disbanded, I also have a responsibility to them to bring them back into the fold so to speak. Josh?"

"Yes, Alpha."

"I believe you have laid claim to your mate?"

"I have. I have claimed Anna as my mate and she has acknowledged my claim in front of witnesses."

A loud round of applause and congratulations went up around the young couple. Some of the wolves from other packs weren't too keen on the idea of the pretty dark-haired girl being paired off so quickly and to one of Dylan's men.

"Then, Josh, as her mate I formally charge you to discipline your mate in such a way and to such a degree that the idea of misbehaving in this manner is something she will refrain from doing in the future."

"No…" Anna cried. The women of Anna's former pack protested and began to struggle anew. They were quickly subdued and quieted.

Darby watched as Nick crossed the room and took her from her two captors.

"You, little girl are about to receive your first taste of discipline as member of Calon Gwyllt. Let's go."

Nick turned to head back to the residence in which she'd been housed. Darby tried to fight him. She jerked back against his strong, restraining grip. She made a fist and tried to hit him with the hand not under his control. Nick's strength was too much for her for her efforts to prove fruitful. He caught the blow she tried to deliver with his other hand.

Darby watched as Nick turned to her, eyes blazing. "Enough. You can either come with me quietly or I'll give you a preliminary spanking right here in front of everyone, toss you over my shoulder, and carry you down to the other house. Once we get there, you're going to strip, spend some time in the corner, and then I'm going to paddle your backside until you can't sit down for a few days."

"If you think you scare me, you couldn't be more wrong. I've been beaten so many times, it no longer has any effect on me. You might be able to make my ass so sore it hurts to sit down, but you won't break me and I will never accept that you and your kind have any kind of authority over me."

Nick took a deep breath. "Whether you accept it or not, you are now a member of this pack and subject to Dylan's authority as your alpha. I'm going to recommend we focus on correcting your behavior. We'll leave it to your new mate to deal with your attitude."

Darby felt herself be half dragged/half marched down to the secondary residence and up to her room. She noted that the guards patrolling the house had doubled and Tim had once again taken his position outside the door. They entered the room and Nick swatted her behind as he propelled her forward.

"Strip and go stand in the corner," he growled.

"No."

She could see that her blatant refusal had taken Nick a bit aback.

"The women of pack Calon Gwyllt knew if they've earned themselves a punishment spanking, it is best to become contrite and accept what is going to be given to them. It's high time you and the rest of girls from Bae Diogel learned the same. No is not an acceptable answer. In fact, the only acceptable answer is 'Yes, Beta' or 'Yes, Nick,' then you do what you're told. Now get yourself naked and go stand in that corner."

Darby raised her chin in defiance. "And I said no. You want to beat me? Go ahead. But I'll be damned if I'll help you or be reduced to being punished like a child."

"That's your final word?"

"Yes."

"Have it your way." Nick crossed the room and headed toward the bed, catching her by the arm and dragging her over his knee as he stripped down her pants. He gave no further clue, said not another word, but began to spank her now bared bottom.

It had been more than two years since anyone had hit her. Darby had almost forgotten how much it hurt and how much she didn't like it. She began to struggle to get away from him. The swats he was delivering to her backside were painful and humiliating at the same time. Darby tried to struggle to loosen his hold to no avail. All she managed to do was make Nick increase the speed and strength of his spanking.

"That behavior is only going to result in you getting a worse spanking. You let me know when you're ready to get up, get undressed, and stand in the corner," he said in a calm, even tone of voice.

"No," said Darby, her voice fighting back tears. It was said Nick had a wickedly hard hand and more important knew how to apply it to its best use.

"Yes." Nick said nothing more but continued to assault her backside with considerable skill and expertise.

Darby could feel every blow he landed. She knew that come morning her bottom would be red and swollen.

"From how quickly you bottom is deepening in color, it's obvious that it's been far too long since you've found yourself over a man's knee receiving the discipline you so apparently needed. I realize now you played me this afternoon and those false tears were just a ruse to lull me into a sense of false security in order to avoid the spanking your earlier nonsense had earned you," Nick said as he continued to land hard swat after hard swat across her ever increasingly sore backside.

Darby finally quit struggling and Nick backed off the intensity of the spanking.

"That's better," he said. "You need to learn that fighting me or your mate will only result in a harsher spanking. Submitting will usually lessen both the intensity and duration."

Darby was having to bite her lip to keep from crying.

Sensing she might be ready to yield, Nick stopped spanking her and asked in a calm tone, "You want to rethink standing in the corner?"

"I hate you. I hate all of you."

"Yes, you've made that clear. But do you want to hate me face down over my knee getting your bottom spanked or would you prefer to do that naked and standing in the corner?"

"If I agree to go to the corner, will you agree not to spank me anymore?"

"No. Right now, you're getting spanked for refusing to do as you were told. After you've had some time in the corner, I'll put you back over my knee and you'll get spanked for that little stunt you and Anna pulled this evening. That spanking, little girl, will most likely involve my belt unless I see a substantial change in your attitude. Now, do you want to go to the corner or should I continue with this portion of your punishment?"

"Fuck you!"

Nick resumed spanking her. "Not an acceptable answer and not something in which I have any interest where you're concerned, but I rather suspect your mate will find having you across his knee highly arousing."

Although he wasn't in the least aroused by spanking Darby, Nick had to admit she had a lovely, round, firm backside. Some man was going to have a mate with a delightful bottom to spank as well as caress.

He continued in a conversational tone, "I've always found that little girls tend to learn their lessons more quickly and better if their spanking is followed by a good fucking from their mate."

"Stop, please!" Darby could no longer hold back the tears. "Please, Beta, stop. I'll go stand in the corner."

Nick smiled but did not laugh. He stopped spanking her. "If I let you up, you're going to remove the rest of your clothing and go stand in the corner, yes?"

"Yes, Beta."

"And then when I'm ready to continue, you're going to come to me and put yourself across my knee and submit to your spanking for your little run this evening, yes?"

"Yes," she whispered.

"Yes, what?" he said, beginning to spank her again.

"Yes, Beta," she cried.

"All right. You can get up. You strip right here in front of me."

Darby pushed herself off his knee and stood before him. He pulled his handkerchief out of his back pocket and reached up to dry her tears. Darby was surprised at his tenderness.

"Take the rest of your clothes off and go stand in the corner like a good girl," he said soothingly.

As much as she wanted to defy him, the set look on his face told her all that would result in was her being spanked further before being made to strip, stand in the corner, and wait for him to finish punishing her.

"If you do as you're told, Darby, and submit to the rest of your punishment, I won't use my belt. If you want to continue disobeying or throw a tantrum, you will have a nice set of welts across your bottom." He reached up and stroked her hair. "Be a good girl, Darby, I'd rather not have to use my belt on you."

She said nothing, but silently removed her clothes and went to stand in the corner. She stood there for several moments, very uncomfortable with the silence between them. "Nick, can I ask you something?"

"If you stay facing the corner and use a respectful tone, yes."

"The wolf who claimed Anna, he'll be kind to her, won't he?"

"Josh is a good man. Yes, he'll be kind to her. He's going to have to discipline her tonight for this little stunt, but more than one good pairing has involved a good spanking along with being marked," he said, smiling as he remembered his own claiming of Bianca.

"I won't go back."

"Back where?"

"To that bastard that marked me."

"No, you won't. Dylan is aware of the abuse you

suffered. He has already begun the work to dissolve that union."

"He won't send me back?"

"No. There isn't a one of us at Calon Gwyllt—male or female—who would see you returned to an abusive mate."

"But won't there be trouble?"

Nick laughed. "Oh, probably. But Dylan doesn't concern himself overly much with such things. The protection of his pack is his chief concern. And you, little girl, are a member of that pack."

Darby continued to stand in the corner with her backside ablaze from the spanking she'd already been given.

"Are you ready to submit to the rest of your punishment?"

Darby took a deep breath and tried to stem the flow of tears that were right behind her eyes. "Nick, please. I haven't been spanked in more than two years. It hurts so badly, please?"

"No, little girl. You have this punishment coming. I let your nasty behavior slide earlier today and I suspect those were crocodile tears I saw at that time. But you are not going to pull a stunt like this again. If you do, regardless of whether you submit or not, I'll take a belt to your backside and welt you good. Are you ready to submit to my authority and to your well-deserved spanking?"

"Yes, Beta," she whispered.

"That's a good girl. You can come out of the corner and put yourself over my knee."

Darby crossed over to him and hesitated. "Please?" She hated that it felt like begging.

Nick shook his head. "No, put yourself over my knee, Darby and submit."

She laid down over his knee. "That's a good girl," he said as he rubbed her already painful backside.

He placed his hand in the small of her back to steady her and once again began to rhythmically and steadily spank her bottom. She tried hard not to squirm or cry. She lost the battle to crying after about the fifth swat.

"That's right, just let it out. I know it hurts. But you were a very naughty girl tonight, weren't you?" he said gently.

"Yes."

He swatted her harder as he made his voice more authoritative. "Yes, what?"

"Yes, Beta," she wailed.

Nick backed off the intensity again. "In this pack, naughty girls get their bottoms spanked by either Dylan, myself, or their mate. But that doesn't mean they won't be forgiven. Are you sorry about the trouble you caused?"

"I'm not sorry I tried to run."

Nick stopped for a moment and considered her answer. "I suppose that's an honest answer and understandable in light of your circumstances. But do you understand that a repeat of this behavior will find you getting an even worse spanking?"

"Yes, Nick."

"Your bottom on fire, little girl?"

"Yes, Nick. Please, no more."

"All right, I think you may have learned your lesson. You can get up, but you go back and stand in the corner. And you don't rub that sore backside until I tell you that you can."

Darby went back and stood in the corner. Nick made her stand for about fifteen minutes and then turned back the bedcovers and told her to come get in bed. Darby did as he instructed and he tucked her in. No one had ever tucked her in before in her entire life. He gently kissed her forehead.

"Go to sleep, Darby, and behave yourself. I don't want to have to repeat this lesson."

CHAPTER THREE

The next morning Darby awoke and uncurled her body from how she'd been sleeping on her side. She rolled over onto her back to stretch but yelped when her weight hit her sore bottom. "Jesus, that hurts. His mate wasn't kidding about not wanting to be put over his knee," she muttered to herself.

There was a discreet knock at the door and Bianca popped her head inside. "Good morning!"

"It was until my ass made contact with the mattress… then good went right out the window."

Bianca nodded. "Trust me, I know the feeling all too well." She grinned. "But in all fairness, I did warn you."

Darby's head snapped up. She was ready to make a nasty retort when she realized Bianca was teasing her, but not to be mean, but rather to commiserate with her. Darby smiled. "Yes, apparently, my hearing was damaged in the run from Bae Diogel. That smells good. What did you bring me? Am I allowed out of my room?"

"Yes. Brunch will be about eleven. I just figured you hadn't eaten since we had wine last night…"

"About that… when we talked, I wasn't planning what we did. I just wanted you to know that I didn't sit here and lie to your face."

"That never occurred to me. I did want to bring you something and to check in with you. As I said, my mate can have a wicked hand. Unfortunately, I know that better than anyone. Seriously, how are you feeling?"

"As I said, my ass hurts but only if I sit on it. And I suppose it could have been worse. He told me if I try it again, he'll take his belt to me. I'm assuming that's worse?"

"And then some. I am also, sad to say, an expert in that as well."

Darby smiled, accepted the mug handed to her, and put the tray down on the bed. There was a rasher of bacon lying next to home-baked bread toasted to a golden brown with plenty of butter and homemade strawberry jam. "Yum! They certainly feed you well here."

"Dylan tries to take care of everyone. This is the best place I've ever been. I've never been happier, but I sure didn't start out that way."

"What do you mean? It's obvious your mate adores you."

She grinned. "Yes, he does. But why I'll never know. My brother, who was the alpha of our pack, sent me here after I'd scared off all the local wolves and become truly unmanageable. He hoped that Dylan would take me as a mate."

"Really?"

Bianca nodded. "But from the moment I got here, Nick knew. So did I, but I didn't want to be mated… especially to a beta. God, I was awful to him."

"But you did agree, right?"

Bianca laughed. "Oh, I agreed and declared myself in front of Dylan and Matthew. Of course, at the time, I was face down over Nick's knee with a naked ass and having his strap applied with considerable vigor to my backside."

"No…"

Bianca laughed again. "Yep. The first time we mated was with me standing in the corner while he mounted me from behind and made sure I understood just which one of us was the dominant one… and that it wasn't me."

"Didn't you hate him?"

"While he was blistering my butt, you bet. My father was overly indulgent as was my brother and he had a weak beta. Was I brought down off my high horse when he chose to spank me into submission in front of Dylan and Matthew instead of making me run? Yes. Did I want to hate him when he mounted me from behind in the corner?" Bianca laughed with the memory of her own foolishness. "I did, but it only lasted until he breached me the first time with his cock. I'd never felt anything as exquisite or sensual in my entire life. When he finished with me in the corner, he took me into his lap and let me cry and rage at him. Then those wicked hands started seducing me. He spent most of that night between my legs showing me just how much pleasure I was capable of. By the next morning I was completely and utterly his. I know you don't want to hear this, but if you do hear your mate call, don't fight it. There's not a pair here at Calon Gwyllt who aren't fated mates. There is something very powerful in knowing your mate cares enough to hold you accountable and will use every ounce of his courage, passion, and power to protect you."

"I'm glad to hear your forced mating worked out," said Darby. "But that wasn't my experience. When I say I'd rather die than go back there, I'm not being melodramatic. I won't do it. I'll find a way to kill myself before I'll take another mate. And I'll kill any alpha who comes sniffing around. I won't endure being knotted ever again."

Bianca reached out and touched Darby's arm. "You don't need to be afraid. Dylan has already started proceedings to dissolve your union with that bastard who mistreated you. He will not see you sent back. And the whole pack is committed to the same. That bastard will never, ever touch you again."

"But the Council doesn't like to dissolve mated pair unions."

"Dylan hasn't given them an option. He has a lot of power in our society. And he's got several powerful packs who will back him."

"Thank you."

"I don't want you upset when you go down to brunch so I thought I'd give you a heads up… both Skylar and Roz were formally claimed last night. After Nick left with you, Dylan and Oliver made claim to them. They both refused, and rather colorfully I might add, and were forced to run. Both returned to the house and declared their vows."

"And, I'm back to hating him. He'll protect me from some guy he doesn't know, but because he wants Skylar he forces her to submit to him? With all due respect, Bianca, our wolf society sucks big time."

"Nick said both Oliver—that's Roz' new mate—and Dylan called for them. Both Roz and Skylar heard their call. I've seen both of them this morning. Skylar seemed very happy and Roz was beaming. Both men are, of course, very proud of themselves."

Tim knocked on the door and stuck his head in. "Bianca, Nick wants you and Darby up at the main house. I'm to take you up the back way."

"Trouble?"

"Could be. That misbegotten bastard who was paired with Darby showed up with that jerk from Atlantic City. You know the one whose nose Josh broke?"

Bianca nodded. "Oh, and Josh formally claimed Anna, but I think you knew that. She too seemed very happy with her mate this morning. Come on, let's go up to the main house."

•••••••

Dylan had returned with Darby's mate and the alpha from Atlantic City as well as a representative of the Ruling Council. Dylan sent Skylar up to get Darby. She explained to her as they came down the stairs what Dylan needed her to do in order to protect her.

"You trust him, Sky?"

"I do. I don't like what he did to tear our pack apart, but I do think he's trying to make the best of a bad situation."

"Your mark looks like it hurt."

"It did. As you know, when an alpha marks you, the wound is much deeper and more permanent than when any other male does it. And partly he was eradicating Micah's mark."

"Doesn't that bother you?"

"No, I understand it. When your alpha marks you, just remember that he's getting rid of the last vestiges of your previous union."

"Sky, I don't want to be mated again."

"Darby, let's get through one thing at a time. Keep in mind, Dylan is making a stand for you. He should just hand you over, but he won't. If he has to, the pack is prepared to fight to keep you. He's worthy to be your alpha."

"But you are my alpha."

Skylar turned her so that she was looking directly at her. "I am no longer anyone's alpha. I am mate to an alpha… to your alpha. Do you understand?"

"You know he had his beta spank me last night. That man has a wicked hand."

"Yes, but he only spanked you. He didn't beat you, right? In a lot of packs it would have been far worse. I'm not necessarily a fan of our male-dominant society, but Dylan does seem to be fair and he does care."

"I don't trust any of them. But I trust you. If you tell me this is what I have to do, then I'll do it."

"It is, Darby. It's the only way we can protect you."

They entered the study. Darby's mate moved toward her. Skylar stepped in front of her and growled.

He jumped back. "See? He hasn't any control over her. She growled at me. She's a woman and she can't growl at me. I demand he punish her and make her apologize."

Darby suppressed a grin. What that toad didn't know

was that Skylar had more than enough bite to back up that growl.

Dylan laughed and moved to stand beside his mate. "That's enough, Sky."

Skylar looked at him in disbelief.

He continued, "I won't have you growling at those who are beneath you."

Skylar smiled.

"Now give me a kiss and behave yourself," Dylan said.

She took his face in his hands and kissed him deeply. "Yes, Alpha."

He kissed the tip of her nose and then bent and kissed her mark. "Do you need something for the discomfort, love? I can have Thomas get you something."

Darby stared in disbelief. She realized they were playacting for the outsiders, but under the act there was true feeling. Skylar had succumbed to the charms of the alpha of Calon Gwyllt.

"Thank you, but no."

He turned to Darby. "This," he said, indicating her mate, "says he is your mate and your alpha and thinks you should be returned to him. What do you think?"

Darby looked at Skylar, who nodded. She took a deep breath and then announced quietly, "He was a cruel and abusive mate. I would ask to call you alpha and put myself in your care."

He turned back to the three uninvited guests. "That settles it, gentlemen. The lady is under my protection. Should you wish to claim her, you may issue a formal challenge and I will answer it." He wasn't quite growling, but the level of his voice and the grumble behind it left no doubt that he was deadly serious.

The other men all backed away. Skylar linked her arm through her mate's. "If he issues a challenge to the death, can I kill him?"

Dylan laughed. "Sky, what have I told you about weapons and threats."

"But he is neither a member of our pack nor a guest. The rule doesn't apply."

He laughed and kissed her. "That's true. What do you say? Care to take my mate on in a fight?"

One of the Council members said, "You need to get her under control."

Dylan advanced on him. "But I do, didn't you hear her ask my permission to kill him?" When the Council member backed away, he returned to her and nuzzled her neck. "Such a good mate. Beloved, why don't you take Darby and see to our other, invited guests. I will show these men to our gate."

Darby had heard that instead of simply auctioning them off, he had gone to the trouble to arrange a weekend house party. The invited guests would include unmated alphas of packs that had either voted with Calon Gwyllt or at least were sympathetic and wouldn't be unkind to any of the women from the rogue pack at Bae Diogel.

Skylar wrapped her arm around Darby's waist and walked out of the study to join the party. Once they were out of hearing, they both burst into laughter.

"Sky, when he praised you for asking permission before you killed him, I had to bite the inside of my cheek to keep from losing it. But I don't want to cause you trouble."

"Don't worry, Darby. We kicked that guy's ass when it was just our household of women. I think he'd fare far worse if he comes back without an express invitation from Dylan himself. Why don't you come and join everyone? Thomas is a wonderful cook. Someone told him my weakness for strawberry blintzes. They are divine."

•••••••

The rest of the day passed uneventfully. As the other women from Bae Diogel had caused no further issues, Dylan allowed that they could leave their residences and roam the grounds either around the houses themselves or with one of his pack members as an escort. They bristled a bit at having their freedom curtailed, but both Roz and Skylar tried to soothe their feelings by repeatedly pointing out they could still be confined to their rooms.

Darby seemed the most distressed and Roz tried to speak with her.

"I don't like it, Roz. I'm glad that you, Sky, and Anna think you can live with these men and find some kind of happiness, but it doesn't negate the fact that you were forced."

"No, Skylar and I had a choice. We chose to run. We just weren't able to outrun them."

"And Anna?"

"She too agreed to become Josh's mate. Have you seen them together? She seems to be quite taken with him and he positively dotes on her."

"I won't agree to be mated again. I won't."

"Then you put Dylan in the position of having to select your mate and if you still refuse, he'll force you to run."

Darby shook her head. "I'll kill any male who tries to take me. I swear it."

"Darby, please, try to calm down. Dylan isn't going to give you to someone who will abuse you."

"He doesn't know that. I won't live that way again, Roz. I won't." Roz watched her walk off with a feeling of dread.

CHAPTER FOUR

The remainder of the week was quiet as the pack of Calon Gwyllt prepared for their guests. Darby was moved up to the main house and remained polite but aloof. Her feelings of anger and resentment grew daily, but she kept them smoldering in private.

•••••••

On Friday morning, Roz and Oliver finally took their leave. Roz had asked her new mate if she could say goodbye to the women of Bae Diogel and he had given his permission. Roz had assured each of them that she was incredibly happy, was looking forward to her new life in the Hamptons, and that Oliver was the best lover she'd ever had. She also went out of her way to make sure all of her former pack mates knew that when done correctly, being knotted and tied to your mate was the best feeling in the world.

•••••••

Jean-Michel was happy to have arrived at Calon Gwyllt.

While he and Dylan had never been close friends, the two alphas certainly knew each other by reputation, respected each other, and had been on the same side of the Council's vote in the matter of how to deal with the women of Bae Diogel.

Dylan's new mate, Skylar, had arranged for an informal BBQ for all of the arriving guests for the weekend house party. Jean-Michel smiled to himself. It was a good strategy to set things up so that both invited guests and the women of Bae Diogel could mingle and get to know one another. Certainly it should make the women feel less like they were being offered up for sale. Jean-Michel was impressed as it seemed the other women of Calon Gwyllt were trying to be supportive and understanding.

Things seemed to be going smoothly until Jean-Michel saw one of Dylan's men rush out of the house, clearly distressed while trying to hide that fact. He watched as Dylan quickly directed his men in an effort to resolve whatever had gone awry.

Jean-Michel suspected it had to do with the women from Bae Diogel as he watched a quiet but heated exchange between Dylan and Skylar. Whatever the cause, Dylan seemed to resolve the matter by giving his mate a brief, discreet spanking and then sending her on her way with his beta, Nick.

Jean-Michel turned to JD, his lifelong friend and the beta of the New Orleans pack. He told him to gather the other two members of the New Orleans pack and join him. Jean-Michel headed off to intercept their host.

Jean-Michel watched as Dylan stepped away from his omega, Matthew.

"Jean-Michel," Dylan said in a falsely hearty voice, "welcome. I hope your accommodations are acceptable?"

"Other than being away from all those beautiful women—both from Bae Diogel and from your own pack—they are lovely."

Dylan smiled. "Yes, I am surrounded by beauty in all its

forms. I'm sorry that my mate is indisposed."

Jean-Michael laughed. "From what I saw, you seem to be the cause of your mate's indisposition."

"Saw that, did you?"

"I see and know most things, my friend. I take it there's trouble? Uninvited guests or naughty girls?"

Dylan chuckled. "The latter. Three of them decided to absent themselves from the party."

"As you know, several of my unmated pack members insisted on joining me. We can be discreet and are happy to be of help."

"That would be most appreciated. Some of my men have already shifted and will pick up their trail. Perhaps you and one of your men could join one group and I could take the other two members of your pack and join the other?"

"Sounds like an excellent division of labor. Lead on," said Jean-Michel as he motioned to his men.

Jean-Michel watched as Dylan's men shifted and picked up the girls' scent. He had brought three of his unmated pack members with him. It was his hope that he would be allowed to take at least two of the girls back with them to New Orleans. His pack was heavily weighted with unattached males. They needed to start bringing females into the pack if they were to remain strong and healthy.

He wasn't opposed to human females being turned, but not unless and until they had given their informed consent. He'd had to oust one pack member for turning a girl without her consent. They had seen her through the change. She had been furious about what had been done to her. She'd left the safety of the pack for a brief interlude but had then returned asking to become one with them. She was now happily mated to another male from the pack and was expecting their first offspring in the next few weeks.

Jean-Michel was jogging after the shifted wolves as they tracked their quarry. There on the wind he thought he got the whiff of something for which he'd been searching for many years. He stopped and scented the wind. Yes, she was here. The faint smell of crepe jasmine mixed with her unique aroma. He smiled. He removed his clothes and smoothly shifted to more readily run down his prey. Jean-Michel began to howl what he hoped would be his last mournful song in search of his mate.

• • • • • • •

Darby heard members of Dylan's pack closing in. The women who had run had separated, hoping at least one of them would be able to get away. Darby stopped and listened intently. She heard the group of wolves trailing them separate into two smaller groups. Darby shifted and headed toward the beach. They had chosen low tide as a time and means to escape from the Calon Gwyllt's estate.

She heard a lone howl and felt it reverberate through her bones. *No. This cannot happen to me. I will not be mated again. I want to be free.* The howl sounded again, changing to a baying sound toward the end. *Whoever he is, he's got my scent. Damn.* She heard the two smaller groups go after Summer and Gina but felt the lone wolf behind her in hot pursuit.

Darby ran, willing herself to find more speed. She could feel her heart pounding in her chest. She heard the mournful song again; it caused her to stagger. The pull to return his call, reverse her course, and find her mate was strong. She shook her head; she refused to heed his siren song. She ran down the incline from the bluff above the beach and down to the dunes.

She had just reached the sand when once again she heard him call. Only this time, she felt the tail end of an alpha roll reaching out to her. He knew she was close and knew she was resisting him. If he got any closer, the alpha roll combined with his song would literally knock her off her feet and he would be on her before she had a chance to recover.

Her paws had barely touched sand when his alpha wave hit her at full force. Combined with the song he continued to howl, Darby had her feet swept out from underneath her. The air was expelled from her lungs and she rolled onto the beach in a heap. Before she could regain her bearing or shift back to human form, the large, powerful wolf was upon her.

• • • • • • •

Jean-Michel felt triumphant. He had her! To feel her so near was sweet… He accelerated and saw the force of his alpha wave hit her, knocking her to the ground. Jean-Michel closed the distance between them and pounced. He grabbed her by the scruff of her neck, pinning her to the ground. Jean-Michel had no desire to mark and knot his mate in her wolf form. He shook her by the scruff as she fought to free herself from his possession. He pressed her into the ground so that she could feel his need. Jean-Michel wanted her to understand that if he chose to, he could mark her and make her his and no one would challenge him. The bitter taste of another alpha's mark filled his mouth. His need to remove it from her body was almost overwhelming.

He shook her again. He felt her yield and shift back to her human form. She was beautiful. Of medium height, she had beautiful pale blonde hair, blue eyes, and a decidedly feminine figure. Her breasts were a bit larger than average with enticing areolas and nipples. She had a lovely, rounded, firm bottom, a small waist, and long, lean legs. Jean-Michel shifted back as well, ensuring that she was still pinned beneath him. He desperately wanted to mark and mate with her, but he could feel both fear and anger emanating from her being. Jean-Michel nuzzled her, inhaling her scent deeply.

He chuckled. "What a naughty mate you are. You heard me calling you, but resisted my call," he said in a pleasant and soothing voice. Darby would later tell him that she thought his voice sounded like molasses.

"I am not your mate," said Darby, shaking from both anger and fear.

He chuckled and nuzzled her again, happy to have finally found her. "Be still, mate. I won't hurt you. Well, I suppose that's not really true, is it? After all I will have to discipline you for both disobeying Dylan and then for not coming to me when I called you. Then there's the matter of ridding you of another's mark and giving you my own. But then, sweet, I will take you to my bed to knot and tie you. I will make you forget how I had to punish you."

He ran his hands down her flanks as he whispered kisses along the back of her neck and her shoulders. How he would have preferred not to have to spank her before they mated for the first time. She, however, had left him little choice in the matter. He would need to see to her punishment for this mischievous little run. She would be mate to the alpha of New Orleans and would come to love her life and him… of that he had no doubt.

His cock was hard and a knot was already forming in anticipation of the night ahead. She struggled against him as it made contact with her naked buttocks.

"Get off me, you bastard." She bucked and struggled, which did nothing to improve her position but did bring her in closer contact with his groin.

He wrapped his arm around her middle and pulled her tighter against his body, while his other hand went up to fondle her breast. He cupped it and squeezed it gently and then rolled her nipple between his thumb and forefinger. His possessive handling of her infuriated her. He rained more kisses along the tops of her shoulders. She continued to struggle and tried to get away from him. He pinned her more closely, rubbing his engorged cock along her buttocks. Jean-Michel knew it was best for her to become comfortable being in close proximity to his cock and the feel of it inside her body. Both her wolf and human form were very appealing to him. He anticipated many hours spent within her warm embrace proving that she was his and his alone.

"Get off and get that thing away from me."

He chuckled. "Before long, you will be well pleased to

have my thing as you so charmingly named it nestled in your wet, silky warmth, stroking you to ecstasy before I force my knot and then tie you to me."

Jean-Michel looked back over his shoulder and saw Dylan, JD, and the other men approaching. Jean-Michel growled a warning to keep clear. His mate was naked—from this point forward he would be the only one to see her in that state. Between Dylan and the other men, the naughty girls who had thought to escape them had been retaken.

"So that's the way it is," said Dylan, grinning.

Dylan had originally earmarked Bae Diogel's omega, Lacey, for the alpha from New Orleans. When they had spoken before Jean-Michel accepted Dylan's invitation, Jean-Michel had confided that he believed that his mate was among the women that had once been the Bae Diogel pack. Dylan had suggested that Lacey, as a proven omega, might be someone he should strongly consider.

Jean-Michel laughed. "I'm afraid the fair Lacey is meant for another," he said to Dylan. Turning to JD, he said, "Did you happen to find my clothes?"

"I did, my friend."

"If you would toss them to me and then all of you turn your backs so my mate may have a little privacy…"

Jean-Michel reached out and grabbed the long-tailed button-down shirt he'd had on. He wrapped Darby's hair around his fist to keep her from running. He handed her his shirt as he helped her to her feet. She struggled but he used her hair to give her a gentle shake as he had when he'd had her by the scruff of the neck. "Put this on, sweet. I'd prefer it if the first time you met some of your new pack mates you weren't unclothed."

"They are not my pack mates and you sure as hell aren't my alpha or my mate." She made sure to say the last part loud enough where all could hear.

"Do not try my patience, mate. I am both; you will submit to me and call me such. If you continue to misbehave in a manner unworthy of your position, you will find yourself over my knee having your first taste of my displeasure with an audience. Now cover yourself."

Darby took the offered shirt and put it on. Once she was sufficiently covered, Jean-Michel pulled her into his embrace, kissing her soundly and holding her close by slipping the hand not tangled in her hair under the shirt and cupping her buttocks. She struggled against him. He rubbed her backside, enjoying both the feel of her bottom and her passion. He patted her lovingly and in order to cup her cheeks more firmly. Jean-Michel smiled as he realized that he would need to accustom her to having his hands on her derriere—for pleasure, discipline, or both.

"Dylan, might I ask you to hold onto my mate while I get at least part of my nakedness covered?"

JD looked at his friend and his engorged cock with the rapidly growing and hardening knot and grinned. "That thing going to fit back in your jeans?"

Jean-Michel looked down. His knot was continuing to swell and becoming decidedly uncomfortable. He longed to have Darby on her back as he mounted her and claimed her fully.

Jean-Michel watched Darby's expression as she got her first glimpse of him. Jean-Michel wasn't as tall as Dylan, but he was well muscled and strong. He knew that his cock was large and well made. He watched as her eyes betrayed her panic upon spying the size of his knot. Jean-Michel knew she had been ill-used by her formed mate and concluded that the man had caused her considerable pain.

"Why do you think I brought my loose-fitting ones?" There was laughter from the men and renewed struggles from the girls. Jean-Michel handed Darby over to Dylan. He quickly pulled on his jeans and boots and took possession of Darby again. He kissed her and said, "I missed you, mate. You were gone too long from my arms."

Dylan smiled. "I take it you are declaring your intention to take Darby as your mate?"

"I am. Apparently it was my Darby's presence and then

her intoxicating scent that called to me." He turned back to Darby, smiling at her. "We have yet to make introductions. I, my beloved, am Jean-Michel Gautier… your mate."

"I will not be mated."

"You will, and we shall be very happily so for the rest of our lives."

"I will shorten your life the first chance I get," Darby growled.

Jean-Michel gave her bottom a hard swat. "Naughty mate. You do not growl at me. We will discuss that further tonight when I am punishing you for your foolishness this afternoon."

"So, you mean to discipline her yourself?" asked Dylan cordially, knowing full well what the answer would be.

"No one but me will ever touch my mate again," said Jean-Michel with a threatening note in his voice.

They turned back toward the house. Dylan and Jean-Michel were in the lead. After Darby rejected taking his hand, Jean-Michel had once again grabbed a fistful of her hair by the nape of her neck to keep her close to him. Dylan found it intriguing that he didn't really seem to mind her trying to dislodge his hand or force him to release her.

"Tell me, Dylan, is my mate always this naughty?"

Dylan laughed. "She's been the most misbehaved of the lot. She also has a nasty habit of encouraging others to join her in her misbehavior. This is the second time she's tried to run."

"I can tell she's a spirited thing, but that isn't a bad trait in an alpha's mate, *n'est pas*?"

"I agree. As you know I took the alpha of Bae Diogel as my mate just recently."

"And yet, it is my mate who causes trouble." He laughed. "Apparently, you've marked and bedded yours to great success."

Dylan laughed with him.

"So, who is the alpha who marked my mate and do I need to deal with him?"

Darby pulled at the hand holding her by the hair. "Let me go. And anything you want to know about me you can ask me, you arrogant sonofabitch."

Jean-Michel stopped and faced his mate. The other men, especially those of his pack, held their breath. Jean-Michel did not release her. He smiled, but some of the amusement had left his eyes. He gently shook her.

"You, my beautiful mate, and I are going to need to come to an understanding about the manner in which you speak to me. Up until this moment you have been disinclined to say anything other than telling me what you will and will not do and calling me names. If you wish to tell me about this man who put his mark on you, you may do so once we're adjourned to our room. I will be happy to listen to anything you have to say to me once we have addressed your misbehavior and nasty attitude… both of which I will curb you of."

"Let go of my hair. You're pulling and it hurts."

"I offered you my hand earlier and you slapped it away. If you would prefer now to walk with me hand in hand, I would be happy to do so. However, you will need to ask me nicely to release my hold of you and walk with me like a good girl with your hand in mine."

"Fuck you!" she spat at him.

He laughed and kissed her. "That too will come after you have spent what I fear will be a considerable amount of time over my knee getting your bottom spanked. As you once again seem disinclined to take my hand, we will continue on as we did before." He turned back toward the house.

Dylan smiled. "She was mated to an abusive bastard. She ran from him—that seems to be her MO when dealing with unpleasant things. He tried to get her back from Bae Diogel and failed miserably. They sent him home nursing his wounds," he said, laughing.

Jean-Michel laughed with him. "They are a spirited group of women. And they wonder why they are so highly coveted as mates?"

"I too find it interesting that they fail to see their desirability. In any event, she lived at Bae Diogel until we had to disband them. He came here to claim her but she declared me her alpha and asked for my protection at my Skylar's suggestion. She has repeatedly told anyone willing to listen that she will not be mated again."

"She has no choice." Dylan nodded in agreement with him. "How did he abuse her?"

"He used to beat her."

Jean-Michel stopped in his tracks and turned to Darby. "Do you wish me to kill him for you and bring you his head on a platter, my beloved?"

Darby searched his face and realized he was deadly serious. "No, that won't be necessary," she said in a meek voice.

"Are you sure? No man worthy of that designation mistreats any woman, but most especially his own. Any man, mated or not, in my pack who does not treat the women of our pack with respect and kindness answers to me."

"And to whom do you answer when you beat me tonight?" she challenged.

Jean-Michel laughed and kissed her. "Naughty mate. I will not beat you tonight. I will turn that pretty bottom of yours a deep shade of red for your naughtiness this day, but never will you suffer abuse at my hands. Would you care to walk hand in hand the rest of the way with me?"

"I suppose it's better than having you drag me by the roots of my hair."

He laughed again. "Then ask me nicely to walk to the house with me and put your hand in mine."

He waited. Darby stood rooted to the spot and once again tried to free his hand from her hair. Jean-Michel did nothing but wait. Finally, she let go of him.

"Would you please release my hair and hold my hand while we return to the house?" she said as she offered him her hand.

Jean-Michel took her offered hand, brought it to his lips to kiss, and then released her hair and put her hand in his. "See, that wasn't so difficult, was it?"

Darby jammed her fist forward, punching him in the mouth. She hadn't had much space and so the blow was ineffectual. Jean-Michel kissed her hand again before tucking it into his arm. She tried to jerk away from him but he held her fast.

He bid a good evening to their host and led Darby up the stairs and into their room.

CHAPTER FIVE

The closer they got to his guest suite, the more Darby tried to hang back. Jean-Michel did not seem to notice. He went to open the door to his—now their—suite and Darby tried to break away. Before she could even turn away from him, he once again had hold of her hair at the base of her neck.

"Naughty mate," he said, chuckling as she struggled against him. "We are going to need to break you of the habit of running when confronted with something not to your liking. Although I must say that while I can understand you wanting to distance yourself from my discipline, I think you will find the pleasure you will receive from me will be something you want to embrace."

"You arrogant jerk."

"Your loving mate," he corrected her. "As much as I'd like nothing better than to get you naked and on your back in our bed, there is the matter of your punishment for today's misbehavior to be seen to."

"You are not going to spank me. And you're sure as hell not going to fuck me."

Jean-Michel chuckled. "That is where you are wrong, *ma choue*. I am your mate…"

"I haven't yet taken any vow… and I won't."

He still held her fast. "Ah, but you will… either voluntarily or in front of witnesses when I force the same from you. But you are my fated mate and you know it. You heard my call and naughty girl that you are, chose to resist me. But in the end, you couldn't… could you?" He ran his hand down on her flank and cupped her bottom. "You are wearing entirely too many clothes."

"All I have on is your shirt."

"As I said, too many clothes." He bent his head and kissed her.

She struggled against him. He held her close, wrapping one arm around her waist and allowing his hand to take up residence on her derriere. He brought his other hand up between them and again cupped her breast before rolling one of her hardened nipples between his thumb and forefinger.

Darby kicked at his shin as she pushed against his chest. His response was to pinch her nipple and swat her backside. She yelped in response.

"That had better be the last time you try to injure me, mate. I will allow that you've had a difficult few days and have never had a mate to hold you accountable."

Before she could protest, he continued, "The bastard who marked you as his abused you—that is not holding one's mate accountable. You will never be abused again. I will now hold you accountable. When I ran you to ground, you became mate to the alpha of New Orleans. You will learn to behave yourself in a manner that fits your position. When you do not, I will punish you."

"As I said, you're an arrogant prick and I despise you."

"Calling me less than loving names, being disrespectful, and lying to me will all result in having your mouth washed out with soap in addition to the spanking you'll be given. I'm going to turn you loose. I expect you to remove my shirt and let me gaze upon your loveliness. If you need some time to compose yourself before I discipline you, you may go stand in the corner. But then, mate, I will see to holding you accountable for your naughty behavior. That will be decidedly unpleasant for you but most likely highly arousing for me… as well as you."

"I won't allow you to beat me. And I would never be aroused by pain or violence."

Jean-Michel chuckled. "Not beat, beloved, spanked. I can tell you are strong-willed and spirited. But my will is stronger and you will learn to yield to it. And the arousal, my sweet, comes not from the pain, but from knowing your mate cares enough to spank you when you misbehave so you can be the best version of yourself. Running away from an alpha who has sworn to protect you, not answering the call of your mate, and not surrendering when you have been caught are all things for which you need to answer. But do not fear, *ma choue*, I have just the cure for the problem of your arousal."

"You bastard."

Before she could even guess his intent, he once again grabbed her hair by the nape of her neck. With the other hand, he stripped her of his shirt and led her into the en suite. He turned on the water and laughed when he saw the soap.

"Having to wash out the mouth of misbehaving females must be a common occurrence. They have goat's milk soap."

Jean-Michel turned on the warm water and soaped his hand. Darby struggled against him, but he held her fast by her hair.

He brought the hand up to her mouth and said, "Open."

She shook her head.

"Naughty mate. When I give you a command, I expect you to obey it. When you don't you'll be disciplined accordingly. Now open."

Darby shook her head again. Jean-Michel rinsed the soap from his hand and moved that hand up to grasp her by the hair. He pulled her forward, bending her over the vanity and giving her ten hard, swift swats on her bottom. She yowled. Nick's hand had been bad enough, Jean-Michel's was far worse. And despite her words to the contrary, she could feel the stirrings of her arousal begin to form deep within her in sharp contrast to feeling nothing akin to that when face down over Nick's knee.

Jean-Michel switched hands and re-soaped his hand. "Open."

Darby was fighting back the tears. The man had a wicked hand.

"Darby, do you want another ten before I force your mouth open and get the job done? Keep in mind, beloved, I am still going to put you over my knee for a proper spanking for your misbehavior today."

Darby tried to respond but the minute her mouth opened to do so, Jean-Michel used his non-soaped hand to immobilize her jaw. His hand entered her mouth and she could taste and feel the soap being transferred. He rubbed the insides of both of her cheeks and the front and back of her teeth. Darby shook her head and brought her hands up to try to pry away the hand that held her jaw open. Jean-Michel continued until the soap that had been on his hand was now in Darby's mouth. When he was done, he took hold of her hair again, rinsed his hand, and gave her a final swat. He took note that her bottom was already showing a bit of color from his discipline.

He led her back into the bedroom and marched her into the corner. "You stay in the corner until I'm ready to give you your spanking." He put her where he wanted her and then gave her a hard swat to her already smarting behind. "If you come out of the corner before I tell you, you will get a spanking just for that. Do you understand?" When she failed to answer, he landed three more sharp blows to her bottom. "Answer me."

"Yes," she whispered as a tear slid down her cheek.

Jean-Michel stroked down her sides and nuzzled her neck. "It will be all right, Darby. You have nothing to fear."

"You're going to beat me. I swore no man would ever beat me again."

Jean-Michel took her by the hand. "Come here, sweetheart." He led her out of the corner and over to their bed where he sat down.

She'd been willing to follow him but once he was sitting on their bed she began to struggle.

"Darby, enough. First, fighting against a spanking you have earned yourself will only get you spanked worse. Second, I just want to talk to you for a minute and want you to come sit on my lap."

He held her hand but did not tug her in his direction. Reluctantly, she complied.

"I am not going to beat you," he said calmly. "I will spank your pretty bottom when you deserve it. But you will always know why you are being punished."

He rubbed her back with one hand and placed the other on her leg with his fingers resting on her inner thigh. Not wanting to look at him, her eyes were riveted to the placement of his hand.

"After I'm convinced you're sorry for whatever behavior got you put over my knee, we will make up. You will enjoy that," he said, smiling. He nuzzled her neck again and kissed her shoulder. "You have no need to fear me."

"I don't want to be your mate. Choose another."

He chuckled. "That's not how it works with fated mates and you know it. We are fated to be together. I will not allow your fear to keep you from being mine." He moved his hand up her thigh and deeper between them. She tried to push it away. "Naughty mate. You do not push my hands away… especially when they are trying to comfort or arouse. Do not do it again. Do you understand?"

She sat still for a moment and then nodded.

"There's my good mate. Are you still afraid?"

"No, but I don't want to be spanked. You already spanked me and it still hurts."

Jean-Michel chuckled again. "Good girl for answering

me truthfully. Unless I'm spanking you for erotic reasons, when I do so I will leave some sting behind to remind you for a day or two that you displeased me to the point I felt I had to punish you. And if you don't want to be spanked, I suggest you learn to do as you're told and behave yourself."

He could feel her body stiffen as she started to rankle against what he'd said. His new mate was definitely a spitfire. He looked forward to bringing her to heel both in and out of their bed. "And who's the arbitrator of whether or not I'm behaving?"

"That would be your mate and alpha… me. Has it been that long a time since you were held accountable?"

"You mean since the bastard beat me? Not long enough."

Darby could feel the anger roll off of him, but oddly enough not at her. "He was no alpha, nor was the bastard that sent you to him in settlement of his gambling debts. I suppose given your past, your fear is understandable. It does not excuse your behavior, but it does make me think that perhaps just the use of my hand instead of warming you up with my hand and then taking my belt to you is in order."

"You'd use a belt on me?" She began to struggle and squirm to get up off him.

He smiled and held her fast. "Yes, beloved, when it is warranted I will take my belt to your bottom and will leave evidence of my displeasure behind in the form of welts. Your behavior in running away from Dylan, inciting two others to go with you, and then failing to heed my call are all things for which a naughty girl should receive a welting."

"No."

"Yes. Have I mentioned to you how truly beautiful you are?" he asked in almost a purr. "You have the most amazing nipples. They're so large and become so erect and responsive. Is your pussy just as responsive?" he asked, dipping his hand back between her legs.

"You'll never know. I swear if you rape me, I'll find a way to kill you."

"I would never rape a woman, any woman, and especially not my mate."

"If you hit me again, I will never agree to be fucked by you, much less have that knot thing jammed up in me so you can pump your cum into me."

"Such crude language from such a pretty mouth. Another area we'll have to work on. But I will tell you this, after I spank you for your naughtiness today, before I mount and claim you, you will beg me to do so."

"I won't," she said, hoping that he could not tell she was becoming more aroused as she was forced to be such close proximity to him.

The steely gaze he gave her was in direct contrast to the grin on his face. "You will, *ma choue*. And come the morrow, your pussy will rival your bottom for discomfort from my use." The steel softened and was once again replaced by humorous glint. "As you seem to have resolved your fear, I think it's time we get your spanking seen to so that I may enjoy the rest of the afternoon between your legs learning how you best like to be loved and mated."

She started to struggle again, but his strength was far superior to her own. He allowed her to gain her feet, but quickly spun her around and pulled her down over his knee. He braced her upper body on the bed itself and used his other leg to trap hers. She tried to flail her arms behind her, but he caught them neatly in his one hand and pinned her. He let her feel that he was in control. She stopped struggling.

"Good girl," he said soothingly as he brought his hand crashing down onto her buttocks.

"You bastard!" she screeched.

"Not true. My parents were happily mated for many, many years. They did not outlive each other by even six months. I don't believe my father wanted to live without her. I never understood that until I sensed you were here."

Jean-Michel began to spank her. If she'd thought the swats he'd given her thus far were painful, the spanking he was inflicting demonstrated a new level of pain. Darby kicked and screamed and tried everything she could think of to get away from him. She even tried going into that dark place she had with her previous mate where nothing he did could touch her. But hard as she tried, she could not escape Jean-Michel's presence or his hand that continued to punish her backside. He focused mainly on the fleshiest part of her cheeks and only placed a few swats to her delicate sit spots.

She endured blow after blow. She screamed, she cursed, and still the spanking continued. All the while he spoke soothingly to her. He reminded her that she was being spanked because she'd been naughty but that when it was over, all would be forgiven and he would bring her great pleasure. Finally, she quit fighting him and went limp over his knee. It still hurt and she could feel every swat.

Darby started to quietly cry. "Stop. Jean-Michel, please stop. I'm sorry."

The minute the words left her mouth, the spanking ceased. "There's my good girl. An apology will always get your spanking mitigated if not stopped. And what are you sorry for?"

"You know."

"I do, but I want to ensure that you know what you should be sorry for. If you refuse to answer, I'll go back to spanking and it'll be at least another ten swats until I think about stopping. Do you want me to resume your spanking?"

"No. I'm sorry for running away from Dylan and for getting Summer and Gina to go with me."

"And?" Nothing but silence answered his question. "Naughty mate." He began once more to spank her.

"God, no! Jean-Michel, please, I'll say it!"

"One—Two—Three—Four—Five—Six—Seven," he counted out the swats. "Eight—Nine—Ten. Now what was it you were sorry for besides disobeying Dylan and causing trouble?"

"I'm sorry I didn't answer your call."

He began to rub her heated and painful backside in a

loving manner. "That's right. You heard my call and resisted coming to me. That was very naughty, wasn't it?"

"Yes," she cried.

Jean-Michel released her and helped her off his knee. He stood with her and cradled her in his arms while she quietly cried.

"I hate you."

"No, you don't," he said, chuckling. "But you'd like to at least right now. I will start to work on remedying that and having you accept your true feelings. Come now, let's get you into bed. The scent of your arousal calls to me."

He could feel her stiffen. "You don't really expect me to just get on my back and spread my legs for you, do you?"

He laughed again. "Yes, my naughty mate, that's exactly what I expect. You can either willingly get in our bed, lie on your back, and let me have my way with you. Or I will put you back in the corner and then fuck you there as the end to your punishment. Perhaps once I've made you come for me three or four times, you will be more agreeable to getting in our bed, spreading your legs for me, and letting me pleasure us both."

He was a most curious man, this new mate of hers. While his face and eyes were shining, there was a core of strength and steel that she could feel herself being drawn to. She knew he would prefer that she acquiesce but would have no problem enforcing his will if she chose to be obstinate.

"What's it to be, mate? Corner or bed?"

"I suppose bed."

He kissed her deeply for the first time, his tongue moving into her mouth to taste her and coax her tongue to do the same. He pulled her close and kept her where he wanted her by placing his hands lightly on her buttocks, causing her to wince and moan.

He had expected her to offer resistance but when all he felt was supple compliance, he whispered, "If you're going to be a good girl, I will let you have a pillow for your backside."

"That's not funny. My ass hurts."

"Of course it does. You just got spanked for being a naughty mate. Just so you know, you're going to feel my loving correction for a few days. Come get in bed, Darby. Let me show you the pleasurable part of being my mate."

He helped her into their bed. He was quite solicitous and made sure she was as comfortable as she could be. He then removed his jeans and boots so he too was naked. He turned back toward her and she glanced down at his arousal.

Jean-Michel saw the panic in her eyes when she saw his fully erect cock. He knew she had been ill-used by her former mate… a fact Jean-Michel intended to make him answer for. He felt that perhaps Darby feared that she could not accommodate him and that he'd force her and that he too would hurt her.

He slid into bed with her and pulled her close. "Do not fear my knot, sweet. You are not ready for that level of pleasure at my hands. Before I knot you, I will have removed your former mate's marking from your body and replaced it with mine."

He eased her onto her back. She was uncomfortable and frightened… understandably so. He began to kiss and nuzzle her, speaking to her in a language similar to French. The hands that had earlier proved to be hard and unrelenting were now soft and sensual. Everywhere they touched her skin, she quivered.

His passion was restrained but palpable. Her body began to respond to his of its own accord. Her nipples had continued to harden until they were now sore and she was quite sure that he would find her dripping with need when he parted her legs.

Darby found he was an excellent kisser and soon was actively participating. His hands began to move down from her head and neck to stroke her back and then to fondle her breasts and nipples. She moaned as he played with her—alternating rolling her nipples between his thumb and forefinger and tugging them with a bit more force.

Once he had his hands on her, the small well of desire his mastery over her during the spanking had created began to grow. He coaxed her body out of the frozen state in which it had existed for so long. Darby could feel the tickle between her legs begin to steadily increase.

He moved his body down hers so that he could suckle and tweak her nipples with his mouth on one breast and his hand on the other. Darby's body came alight with response and she arched her back, pushing her breast more deeply into his mouth.

As he continued to play with her breasts, one hand stroked down her body until he parted her legs and with it her lower lips. In Darby's experience, nothing good had ever come from anyone being around or playing with her most feminine spots. She began to become uncomfortable and tried to push him away.

Jean-Michel growled at her. "What did I tell you about pushing my hands away?" When she failed once again to answer him, he pinched the nipple with which he'd been playing.

"That hurts, Jean-Michel."

"It was supposed to. Did you not hear my question, mate? Were you so lost in your own passion that you couldn't formulate an answer?"

"No."

"Then answer me. What did I tell you about pushing my hands away?"

"Not to do it."

"That's correct. This is the last time I will give you a warning. Do it again and you'll find yourself across my knee for some additional discipline. If you don't like something I do to you then you may tell me after we're done, but you don't just tell me no. Do you understand me?"

"Yes," she said sullenly.

Jean-Michel laughed at her and went back to using one hand to fondle her breast while his mouth captured the other and increased her arousal level substantially. She wanted to resist him; wanted to deny that he was rekindling a part of her she had long thought dead. He moved his hand down her body, stopping to massage her pelvic area just above her mons. When he felt her relax, a single finger made its way through the blonde hair at the apex of her thighs and found her clitoris. He touched it and she moaned loudly. She put her hands on his as if to push him away again. This time when he growled, she moved one hand up to grasp his forearm and the other she left on top of his, putting pressure on his hand to rub her harder.

He continued to lay claim to her body as he watched anxiety give way to arousal and pleasure. When he moved his hand past her clit to her velvety opening, he could feel her thighs relax and allow him greater access to her core. He slid a finger up into her. As he did so, her hips arced up to take him more deeply. Jean-Michel began to stroke her first with one finger and then with two. She was incredibly wet.

Jean-Michel watched as Darby closed her eyes. He felt her hips begin to move in rhythm to his fingers stroking her inner walls. He smiled as he realized she was fast losing her grip on reality. Instead she was being consumed by the web of sensuality he was weaving. He wondered if she'd ever experienced the level of sensuality she was obviously capable of feeling. He could feel the electricity of her desire playing across her skin.

Jean-Michel ceased fondling her breasts and propped himself up on his elbow to be able to more fully enjoy watching her succumb to her passion. He nuzzled her neck and whispered in her ear telling her how beautiful she was, how he adored her, and how happy their life would be together. He doubted the words registered as she seemed intent only on the sensations he was creating by fingering her.

Her breathing became more shallow and lost its depth and rhythm. Jean-Michel could feel as the well of her desire began to gather and center in her core and then to spread throughout her whole body. All she could do was feel his fingers deep within her stroking and coaxing long-held dormant sensations to life.

Jean-Michel pumped her harder and faster and then added his thumb playing with the nub between her legs. The touch there was her undoing. Her pussy spasmed around his fingers, her toes curled and she arched her body in response. She climaxed, grinding her groin against his hand. She opened her eyes and looked at him in wonder. He removed his fingers from her sheath but left his hand resting between her legs.

"Has no man ever pleasured you, my beloved?"

"Nothing like that," she whispered. "Once in a while in the past year or two I've been with a human, but no, nothing like that. Will it always be like that?"

"No," he said and then laughed at the look of disappointment on her face. He leaned down and kissed her. "It will get better."

He rolled over on top of her, putting his knees between her thighs, and kissed her mouth. His tongue stroked the inside of her mouth the same way his fingers had stroked her sheath. He rose from her body and began to rain kisses down her torso. He stopped to suckle her nipples and then to suck the entire areola surrounding them. Without thought she bowed her body to push her breast deeper into his mouth. She grasped his forearms and writhed beneath him. He took the time to ensure both nipples were fully engorged and her arousal reawakened. This time when he reached between her legs, she offered no resistance. As he settled himself so that his mouth would now be able to pleasure her, she stiffened.

"Please, no. If you have to shove your cock in me, just do it."

He chuckled, which caused her to try to squirm away from him. His muscular arms wrapped around her thighs and holding her lower lips parted for him prevented that. She struggled to get away, but he held her fast. Jean-Michel could feel her body at war with her emotions and memories.

He could see and smell her arousal. He had felt its abundance come to life under the ministrations of his fingers. He vowed to help her body's needs conquer her painful memories.

"Remind me to work with you on your pillow talk, beloved. It could use some work. Did you forget that I told you that before I mounted you that you would beg me to do so?"

"That won't happen."

He lowered his head. Right before sucking her clit into his mouth, he murmured, "Ye of little faith." As he wrapped his tongue around her and sucked, her hips surged up. Darby felt her body's desire for him spiral out of control. Her pussy ached with emptiness but began to pulse in need of him. As he sucked the nub between her legs, she felt another orgasm crashing down upon her and cried out. He allowed her to experience its full power. As she relaxed he began to suck and nibble on her again. Now when she squirmed it was not to get away from him.

Darby experienced her second climax in a haze of feeling centered solely on his mouth and what he was doing. She vaguely recognized that her hips were moving in rhythm to his ministrations. With his mouth full of her, Jean-Michel could only make encouraging noises, but that seemed to reassure his mate; she reveled in her pleasure.

Jean-Michel nuzzled her clit and kissed it lovingly. He turned his attention to her molten core, which was dripping with her desire. He plunged his tongue into her to taste her sweet honey and was rewarded when she again pushed herself against his face. Jean-Michel lapped up her honey as she continued to produce more. He thrust his tongue up into her and swirled it around. He could feel her inner walls clamping down and pulsating a deep and old rhythm. Jean-Michel ached for her and he repressed the knot that desperately wanted to form. He longed to replace his tongue with his cock and plunge in and out of her.

Darby clutched at his head. While earlier she wanted

only to be away from him, now she wanted to pull him closer. She had never experienced such a pleasure in the arms of any man, much less an alpha male. His only intent and goal seemed to be to see how much pleasure he could elicit from her at his hands, tongue, and cock. Once again, her breathing became shallow and electricity flowed throughout her. She could feel her pussy spasm as she climaxed again, crying out his name.

When she'd come back to him, she looked down to see him still cradling her thighs between his arms and his chin resting on her mons as he grinned up at her. She couldn't help but smile back at him. While she'd experienced some sexual pleasure, and even orgasmed by her own hand, never had a man brought her anywhere close to that level of sensuality or gratification.

Jean-Michel idly played with her nipples and clit. Slowly he traced circles around them with his fingertips. Her body once again began to respond to his fondling and teasing. Darby closed her eyes and enjoyed the carnal pleasure he was providing. She didn't think about anything just indulged in the sensations he was causing. She could feel the beginning of another orgasm.

When he suddenly stopped, she opened her eyes to once again see him grinning at her. "Why did you stop? I liked that."

He smiled. "Yes, I could see that. You, my mate, are a very responsive woman. That those who came before me did not use you to your full potential is shameful for them. But you should know, my beautiful, sensual mate, that for me that was only the beginning—merely a way to get you completely aroused."

"There's more?" she asked.

Jean-Michel kissed his way back up her body. "So much more."

"I never… I mean, not with a man…"

He kissed her as he chuckled. "I got that feeling as I was enjoying you being pleasured. What would you think if I told you there was even greater pleasure to be had with my cock stroking where my tongue and fingers just did?"

"The knot…"

"Should not concern you, beloved. I have been suppressing it and will disregard my need to allow it to swell again and bury it deep within you. You have been ill-used in that regard; that will not be the case with me. Other than spanking that pretty bottom of yours, have I done anything to hurt you?"

She shook her head. Once again, he put his hand between her legs and began to stroke her. With each successive climax, her body found its way back to that pinnacle more easily and quickly. He backed off his stroking, removing his hand from where her pleasure was centered. He enjoyed that instinctively she knew she wanted more. This time when she pushed at his hand it was to direct it back between her legs.

"Jean-Michel? Please?"

"Please what, beloved."

She pushed at his hand. "Pleasure me."

"No."

"Why?"

He seemed to suddenly change his mind and pressed his thumb against her clit as he began to pump his fingers inside her. She was almost ready to climax when he stopped. She screamed in frustration. "You bastard!"

He laughed. "Again, beloved, we must work on your pillow talk. Would you like me to give you another orgasm?"

"Very much."

"Then ask me to mount you. Ask me to claim your pussy as mine." He could see the fear creep back in her eyes. "I will not knot or mark you until you wish me to do so. You liked when my fingers were inside you stroking you, yes?"

She nodded.

"Then imagine if something that would fill you more completely was doing the same."

"You won't force the knot?"

He nuzzled her and smiled, vowing to kill the man who had so abused her that she feared what should bring her the greatest joy as his mate. "No, my sweet. And if you look you can see that it has gone down since I brought you to our bed."

She looked down. The knot had gone down in size, but his cock was hard and looked uncomfortable for him. But, she believed him when he said it was capable of bringing her even more pleasure. "Jean-Michel?"

"Yes, *ma choue.*"

"Mount me," she whispered, kissing him of her own accord for the first time.

"Do not fear, mate. My cock will only bring you pleasure… even when you don't want it to."

As she giggled, the fear left her eyes and he rolled over on top of her. Her thighs parted easily for him to settle between them. Slowly he breached her opening and sank into her. The knot, while still present, had lost most of its size and rigidity and she barely noticed when it too entered her body.

Darby realized he hadn't lied. His tongue and fingers had provided her with great erotic pleasure. His cock took that pleasure and amplified it. She felt full of him and felt her entire pussy being stroked from its entrance to its end. His length was complemented by girth and her entire circumference was being stroked in the most exquisite way. Her eyes rolled back in her head and she almost orgasmed beneath him before he took his first stroke. He grasped her hips and began to thrust in and out of her slowly. As he thrust forward the third time, he was gratified as her body came undone beneath him and she climaxed for him again, grasping at his arms. He stilled within her and let her ride the crest of her orgasm without being distracted by anything. When her body stilled, he began his slow stroking again.

She wrapped her arms around his neck and whispered in his ear, "Faster. Harder." She wrapped her body around him and flexed her fingers into his back. "More."

He chuckled, delighting in her need. "You, wench, do not tell me how to fuck you. But trust that I will do so until you are exhausted and sore from my attentions."

He continued to stroke her slowly but deeply. Jean-Michel enjoyed how she responded to him. He could feel that she no longer thought to withhold any part of her response.

"Jean-Michel, please?"

He stopped.

"No," she wailed.

"Now that I have you where I want you, my naughty mate, let us come to an understanding. You are my mate. I will give you some time to declare it on your own. If you don't, I'll bring witnesses into our room and force you to declare either on your back or face down over my knee."

He began to move hard against her. She lost track of time and space, all she could do was feel. He had captured her completely. She could do nothing but respond to him. She knew that he was deliberately taking his time in satisfying himself. His only thought seemed to be how long and hard he could pleasure her before succumbing to his need to drive deeply and release himself into her. As he continued to move within her, Darby's pussy began to pulse in rhythm to his stroking. Her hips moved in rhythm to his as much as he would allow. She felt another orgasm begin to well up and envelop her as he stroked harder and faster and finally thrust home to empty himself deep within her.

Darby had always wanted the men she'd been with to get up and leave when they finished with her. But she clung to Jean-Michel. "Don't leave," she whispered, hating herself for her weakness.

He nuzzled her and showed no inclination to go anywhere. "I will never leave you unless they are putting one of us in the ground." He slowly slid from her body and rolled over on his back next to her. He gathered her close, tucking her in under his shoulder and encouraging her to rest her head on his chest. "Sleep while you can, beloved. My cock will recover after a bit and I will take you again."

He held one of her hands in his and rested his other arm protectively on her hip with his hand gently cupping her bruised and swollen ass. She settled against him and listened as his breathing deepened and he began to sleep.

She stayed where she was and let her silent tears fall. When they were over, she wiped them away with her free hand. She had barely fallen asleep when she felt her mate's cock start to harden. He nuzzled her and began to kiss her. He ran his hand down between her legs and smiled when he found the small pool of her nectar at the entrance to her core. "Again?" he questioned quietly.

She nodded and rolled over on her back, wincing as her bottom made contact again with the mattress. He chuckled at her discomfort. "Bastard," she hissed quietly.

"Mate," he corrected as he parted her thighs with his own and without any foreplay, drove into her again. This time as he sank deep, she arched up, surprising both of them with the strength of her response and her climax. "Good, mate."

Once again, he held her hips in his hands to still her from moving with him. Jean-Michel needed her to learn from the beginning that he dominated in all areas of their life, including her sexual pleasure. He rode her hard and long the second time. This time when he emptied himself within her, she was exhausted. As he withdrew from her body, he kissed her deeply and pulled her back into his embrace.

"Do not cry, beloved. I will ensure that no one but I ever causes you pain again."

"I'm not crying," she said.

"But you were earlier."

"How could you know that? You were asleep."

"The men of our pack are very sensitive to our mates. There is little a naughty girl can keep secret. Rest. I will have need of you again this night before we sleep. I have to leave you to go down to join our hosts for dinner."

"Am I not going with you?"

"No. Naughty mates are confined to their rooms. I will have food brought up to you. If you behave while I'm downstairs, you can return to the party for breakfast."

"I would rather go downstairs."

"I'm sure you would. But when you misbehave you often don't get to do things you wanted. You will remain up here."

Jean-Michel watched with fascination as she bristled and her anger reared its ugly head. "So, you'll have need of me after you return?"

He laughed. "Yes. So, rest while you can."

"You're off to enjoy yourself and I can't leave the room. You expect me to just sit here and wait for you and then flop on my back and spread my legs for your use? That's not fair and I'm not going to put up with it."

Jean-Michel kissed her, letting her feel his strength. "Enough, Darby. You will do as you're told and remain up here. There's a man outside the door, and one under the window. Do not think to run from me. If you do, I will not be as understanding as I was earlier this afternoon. When I return, your behavior while I'm gone will determine whether I make love to you or spank you again before doing so."

CHAPTER SIX

Jean-Michel took a shower and got dressed to go downstairs. Darby was curled up in the window seat ignoring him. He walked over to her and stroked her hair. She pushed his hand away. He responded by bringing her off the window seat, sitting down, and pulling her across his knee.

"Naughty mate. Haven't I warned you about pushing at my hands when they stroke you?" He quickly spanked her ten times as she tried desperately to get away from him. His hand reignited the heat he had created earlier when spanking her. "Answer me, Darby."

"Bastard."

"Mate. Answer me or do you need another reminder?"

"No," she said quickly. "I'm not to push your hands away."

"Good girl." He stood and grinned as he saw her nipples were quickly hardening with arousal. He leaned down to give each of her nipples a quick kiss. "Give me a kiss."

She stood naked in his arms. She truly despised him and her body's response to him. Her nipples were getting hard and she could feel she was getting wet. He quirked his eyebrow at her; the question and threat of another quick spanking did not need to be verbalized.

"Fine," she said and kissed him. She'd meant it only to be a light pressing of her lips to his, but he caught her behind her head and pulled her close so he could deepen the kiss. She hated the way her body acted in response to his physical presence.

When he'd finished his leisurely plundering of her mouth, he let her step back. He was grinning from ear to ear. She deliberately drew the back of her hand across her mouth.

He shook his head and laughed. "Naughty mate. I will address that behavior tonight when I return. I will have something sent up to you."

"I don't want anything but to get away from you."

"But you will never get away from me. We are fated mates. I will always find you. And remember what I told you. Run from me and resist my call? You will find yourself with a welted bottom for your trouble. Now be a good girl. I look forward to having the wanton vixen I had beneath me earlier present when I return."

Jean-Michel crossed the room and went out the door, locking it behind him. Darby looked around and could only find his clothes. She slipped the shirt back on and went back to the window seat.

•••••••

Jean-Michel stopped in the kitchen on his way to where the guests were gathering. He spoke quickly with Dylan's excellent chef, asking him to ensure that the two men guarding Darby were fed. He asked that Darby be given whatever she wanted.

His men and his mate's needs seen to, he joined the others. He made his way to Skylar to introduce himself and to assure her of his mate's well-being. He also asked to speak privately with Dylan and Skylar after the party broke up.

His beta, JD, had spoken with him at dinner and told

him that he felt called to Megan. When Jean-Michel had congratulated him, JD had reminded him that the girls of Bae Diogel were to go to different packs and to alphas if at all possible. Jean-Michel had laughed and reminded him that their pack had been kidnapping willing women for hundreds of years and that he saw no reason to stop now if the need arose.

After dinner, Skylar offered to show him to Dylan's study. He followed her into the study and closed the doors behind him.

"Let us be honest with each other," Jean-Michel said, hoping to allay her concerns. "You are not happy about any of this, save maybe finding your own mate. You are concerned for your girls and most likely at this moment for my Darby."

"How honest would you like me to be?"

He laughed. "As honest as you want. This conversation and the way it is delivered goes no further than me."

"Then yes, I'm quite concerned about Darby. The bastard she was previously mated to beat her repeatedly. You should have taken care with how you disciplined her. Did anyone tell you any of her background?"

He chuckled, shaking his head. "Not until this afternoon. I know that the bastard to whom she was mated before beat her. Dylan sent detailed dossiers on each of the girls to those of us who were invited. I must confess, I only scanned them. Having gone back and read Darby's, there is mention of her abuse. But she is not the delicate, traumatized victim you would make her out to be. She took her spanking quite well. Oh, she kicked and cursed and carried on like you girls are wont to do, but she never showed an ounce of fear. She knows she deserved to be spanked for her little escapade this afternoon. She heard me call to her. She ran anyway. She is my life mate. Seeing that bastard's mark on her is repugnant to me, but I know being marked by me is repugnant to her so I would ask for your insight on whether or not to mark her tonight as my own."

"And if I were to tell you that she would hate you forever if you forced your mark on her?"

He laughed again. "I would tell you that was impossible. No one can hate me for long if I choose to be charming. And I assure you, I will use all of my charm on my mate. She said it would not, but I would ask you, would it make her heart more at ease to know the bastard who harmed her was dead?"

"Would you kill him for her?"

"Within the space of a heartbeat."

After a brief discussion that Jean-Michel found informative, Dylan joined them. "My apologies for keeping you waiting. I see my mate has been entertaining you."

"Enlightening as well as entertaining. You are well matched to your mate, my friend. She will be an excellent addition to your pack as my Darby will be to mine. To that end, I wondered if you had given any thought to placing another of your girls within my pack? I thought perhaps with a member of her former pack, it might make transitioning back into a more traditional pack easier for her."

"The Ruling Council wouldn't care for it, nor would a number of the men here. As it is there aren't enough to go around." Dylan leaned over and kissed Skylar. "And I know, your girls aren't candy to be passed around. But you didn't find the rest of them objectionable, did you?"

"No; quite the contrary, with the exception of that rogue from New Orleans, they seemed a rather likeable lot," Skylar said.

"You wound me, mistress," Jean-Michel laughed.

Dylan chuckled as well. "I can't get them right all of the time." Then he sobered. "Did you have anyone in mind?"

"I would be open to any of them. They're all lovely. Some a bit more spirited than others, but nothing that we can't handle. I brought three of my unmated men with me but have another five at home." He smiled. "I must say that all three of the men with me have expressed a strong interest in being gifted with any of these girls, but one I think may have heard a calling."

"Your beta?"

Jean-Michel nodded. "Indeed. I would choose to see him mated. As you well know, a strong beta is an alpha's best asset notwithstanding a beautiful mate. And the strongest beta is one well mated."

Skylar laughed at him. He grinned at her. "But a good beta keeps his alpha safe."

"But what is safety compared to her who loves you and keeps you warm at night?" asked Jean-Michel in a voice dripping with honeyed molasses.

Both Dylan and Skylar laughed out loud. Dylan turned to Skylar. "Darby doesn't stand a chance. He'll win her over in no time."

Skylar nodded in agreement. "So, who has he set his eye on?"

"Megan."

Jean-Michel made his case for his beta being allowed to take Megan as his mate. Dylan asked leave to discuss the matter with his mate as well as the ranking members of his pack. Jean-Michel was not unaware that allowing this might well cause Dylan trouble.

Jean-Michel went to find JD and apprise him of the situation. They were out on the patio and saw one of Dylan's men fetch Megan to his study.

JD immediately became concerned.

"Have a care, *mon ami*," said Jean-Michel. "If Megan answers them truthfully, I am confident we will have their blessing. And if not, we will simply abscond in the night with our mates and they are welcome to visit us in New Orleans."

JD laughed. "You really do have pirate blood in you!"

Jean-Michel smiled. "I do indeed. But I wish they would get on with it. I feel my mate needs me."

"Are you that far gone that you can't be parted from her?"

"Partly, yes. But more to the point, she's up there alone in our room. She's already proven capable of slipping her leash."

"Perhaps you should have left her naked and tied to your bed."

"The thought does have a certain appeal. But I'm trying more to persuade her rather than force the issue."

"And you paddling her backside… is that your idea of persuasion?"

Jean-Michel laughed. "As a matter of fact it is… and it worked very well, I spent a most enjoyable afternoon between my mate's thighs hearing her call my name. Gods, is there anything sweeter?"

"No, my friend. I am very happy for you. I only hope…"

His thought was interrupted by Matthew, who was searching for them. "Dylan would like to see you both in the study."

Both men accompanied him back to Dylan's study. JD looked visibly concerned until they entered the room and Megan beamed at him and flung herself across the room and into his arms.

Jean-Michel laughed and clapped his hands together. "I take it, my friend Dylan, that you have granted my request to allow my pack to claim two of the lovely ladies from Bae Diogel?"

"I think it's that or they run off together."

"God, I'd hate to have to look for another beta. This one has had my back since we were boys." He turned to Megan. "I take it the idea of being mated to this great sot you have your arms around is not totally reprehensible to you?"

"No, Alpha. Thank you."

"Jean-Michel, little one. And 'tis my pleasure to welcome you into our family. Dylan, would you like to make an announcement in the morning and have them wait until then to have JD claim her?"

"No, Jean-Michel. I would have the girls that were of Bae Diogel know that if their heart is called to someone here, I would see them happily mated."

JD disengaged himself from Megan. He approached Dylan. "Thank you. I will keep her safe and well loved."

Nick laughed. "You should also see her well spanked. Don't let her fool you, she did not exactly settle in without a fight, did you?" he said, grinning at her.

"Perhaps it was the wrong beta who was trying to tell me what to do," she teased.

Skylar excused herself and went to find something with which to celebrate. As they left the study, Jean-Michel said, "Do not worry about the shift you were to take this evening, my friend. See to your mate's well-being… and see her marked. It may make some of the alphas accept your pairing more easily."

JD embraced his friend. "I have no words, Jean-Michel."

"That's because none are needed." He leaned down and kissed Megan on the cheek. "Best you learn to mind your mate."

Megan took his hands in hers and rubbed her cheek along them. "Yes, Jean-Michel. I won't give you cause to regret this. Thank you."

He smiled and watched them head to JD's room. He turned back to his own, anticipating the night ahead. He began to suppress the knot that had formed. Normally it would be difficult for an alpha to fight both the need to mark his mate and to bury his knot deeply within her, but for now, the need to reassure Darby that she was his beloved and not just a vessel for his pleasure was his most pressing need.

He greeted his man outside the door to his suite and sent him to bed, assuring him that he would handle his feisty mate now that he had returned. Jean-Michel opened the door and immediately felt and smelled the ocean breeze through the open window and saw that the sheets had been knotted together to make a rope. He couldn't decide whether to laugh or rage at her ingenuity.

He crossed the room quickly and looked out. She had

not made it very far. She had the makeshift rope she was using gathered up around her, only letting it out as she needed to scale down the wall. Jean-Michel took hold of the other end and began to pull her back in, shouting to his man on the ground to guard the ground in case she jumped and tried to make a run for it.

Darby wailed "No!" as Jean-Michel began to reel her back in. Once he had her safely in the window and the window locked, he turned to her.

"Naughty mate. What did I tell you about trying to run from me?"

"I hate you and I will escape from your clutches."

In spite of his annoyance with her attempt to leave him, he couldn't help but laugh. "My clutches? You are a most entertaining mate, even when I'm not enjoying myself by making use of all you have to offer," he said as he ran a finger down her body from the hollow of her throat to just above the apex of her thighs.

"Don't do that," she said and slapped at his hand as her nipples hardened in response.

The smile on his face told her that her response had not gone unnoticed.

"And now in addition to having to punish you for your foolishness with the window, it seems we will have to revisit you pushing or slapping my hands away when I choose to touch you. You, my mate, will find that even an aborted attempt to flee will result in a welted bottom for you."

"No."

"Yes. Take my shirt off and go stand in the corner."

"No, Jean-Michel."

"Did you think that I would not punish you for going out a window on a makeshift rope, which could have caused you grievous injury?"

"I didn't really think about it."

"Well, a good welting should ensure that you'll think before acting foolishly in the future. I told you to get naked and go stand in the corner. I will not tell you again without you incurring additional punishment." He pointed to the corner. "Go."

Darby was finding it hard to reconcile the stern man before her with the man who had brought her so much pleasure earlier in the day. She walked forward and mimicked his gesture of running her finger down his body. She smiled seductively.

"Isn't there something you'd rather be doing with me?" she said as she moved closer to him and offered her mouth to his.

He bent his head and kissed her deeply, enjoying both the taste of her and her response. She wrapped her arms around him and molded her body to his. His body responded as his already hard cock began to throb. He wanted nothing more than to sweep her up in his arms, take her to their bed, and make love to her for the remainder of the night. However, he knew that she needed him to be strong enough to correct her behavior regardless of how much he wanted her.

As their mouths parted, she was smiling. That was her undoing. He knew that she believed she could seduce her way out of a punishment. He would need to prove her wrong. He began to slowly unbutton her shirt. She purred and nuzzled his neck and brought her hands up so she could bring his mouth back to hers.

He slid her arms out of the sleeves of his shirt and removed it from her body. Once again, his beautiful mate was naked in his embrace. He ran his hands possessively over her buttocks. She winced slightly but rubbed herself along his groin. He growled low in his throat. She was a seductive minx.

He grabbed a handful of her blonde hair, tilting her head back. "I can't wait to bed you again, mate, but let us first see to your welting."

"Wh… What?"

He chuckled. "Does my mate think so little of me that she believes I would forego her need for correction to see to my own needs? Fear not, my beloved, I am no such man. Your need for me to prove my love and devotion by seeing to your punishment before seeking my own pleasure will not go unmet."

He walked toward their bed. Once he sat down on its edge, he pulled her struggling body across his knee.

"No, Jean-Michel. You can't do this to me."

"I can and will." He brought his hand down on her already sore bottom.

"You bastard!"

"Mate!" he corrected her. He continued to spank her—harder with each strike. She thrashed and kicked, trying to get away, but again could not get away from him. "I warned you earlier that if you tried to run from me, I would welt your backside for your trouble. I do not make idle threats."

He spanked her with both care and strength. Her already sore bottom colored more deeply and swiftly than it had this afternoon. Heat radiated over her entire backside. Again and again he struck the fullest part of her cheeks. Her bottom bounced under his hand. The pain he was inflicting increased as he continued to spank her. She squirmed and struggled, trying to get away from him, but it did no good.

Darby realized that her fighting him was futile. She longed to be able to go to that dark place where nothing could touch her. She was beginning to understand that somehow, she was joined to Jean-Michel and that she might never be parted from him while she drew breath.

Jean-Michel could feel her surrender to his punishment. He stopped striking her bottom and allowed her to catch her breath as he rubbed her backside. She began to cry, silent tears of anguish. It was all he could do not to gather her in his arms and make love to her to assure her of his heart and her place within it.

"I hate you," she said softly.

"No, mate, you do not. In time you will be able to admit as such, but for now I will take no offense at your words given in grief at what you think you have lost."

"I have lost everything…"

"You have lost nothing, my beloved, and gained everything. The sooner you allow yourself to believe that and embrace your new future, the sooner our time on our bed will be spent in more pleasurable pursuits."

Darby felt his hands leave her body and hated that she longed for them to remain. She heard him unbuckle his belt and the belt slide from its loops.

"No, Jean-Michel, please."

She started to get up but was stopped when he put his one hand on her upper back, gently pushing her back down.

"No, mate. I promised you a welting should you try to run again. You not only tried to run away, but you could have seriously injured yourself with your thwarted attempt to do so out the window. I cannot allow you to continue these foolish stunts of yours."

"Jean-Michel, please don't. He used to use a belt on me. He beat me so hard that I could barely move and it took my back weeks to heal."

Jean-Michel growled in his throat. His mate might not want her former mate dead, but he did. He would see to it once he had Darby settled in New Orleans with him.

"You will never be beaten. Spanked, yes, when you misbehave and welted when it is deserved, but only on your pretty bottom. And you do have a lovely bottom. But you need to learn that when I tell you something, you can believe it. I understand you are afraid, but you need to learn to trust that while I may punish you for misbehavior, you will never be harmed again."

"You bastard."

He laughed enjoying that her spirit had returned. He far preferred the spitting wildcat over his knee. "Mate. You are going to learn to use my proper designation when referring to me. Either mate or alpha." She began to try to wrestle away from him. He swatted her once more with his hand. "Settle down, Darby. I am going to welt you. But if you behave and accept your correction, it will only be five.

Continue to fight, and I will give you a full ten."

"I will never forgive you."

"I am doing nothing that needs your forgiveness."

"You're going to deliberately give me welts."

"Yes, for misbehaving after I specifically told you that I would should you choose to misbehave again. I do not want to have to keep you under lock and key, but I will do so until you show me that you have accepted that we are fated mates and will cease trying to flee. Do you want to accept the five strokes or do you need me to give you all ten?"

"I hate you."

"You do not. Choose, Darby. If you don't, I will choose for you. I will assume that you need the full ten to assure you of my devotion."

"All right, you win. Just the five."

"Good girl. See? That wasn't so difficult. Such a pretty bottom, I hate to have to lay welts across it, but you need to learn before you injure yourself."

Without any further warning, he brought his belt down across both of her butt cheeks. She screamed in fury as much as in pain. Jean-Michel did not wish to draw out her punishment and delivered the remaining four in rapid succession. Darby writhed as each strike wrapped across both of her butt cheeks and laid down a line of fiery agony. Darby was spent and crying when he'd finished. He gathered her up and brought her into his lap where she collapsed against him and allowed him to comfort her.

"I know, mate. I wish you had chosen to behave so that I did not have to do that to you. If there is a next time, I will not be as lenient. I should make you go stand in the corner and think about why choosing to behave is always a better idea than choosing to be naughty."

He rocked her in his arms, cradled against him. He stroked her back and held her, murmuring words of comfort and love to her until her crying stopped.

"Feel better, mate?" he asked softly.

"I hate you."

Instead of getting angry, he laughed out loud. "At some point, mate, I'm going to take offense to that and you'll find yourself with a mouth full of soap to go with that sore bottom."

He reached up and took her nipple between his thumb and forefinger.

"No," she said, hating that her nipple was responding as was the rest of her body. She prayed that he would not put his hand between her legs. She was highly aroused and she was drenched.

Jean-Michel leaned her back and took her nipple into his mouth, sucking and nipping it lightly. He smiled as she moaned in pleasure. She began to struggle anew as he reached down between her thighs and stroked her clit, chuckling at the sharp intake of her breath. His finger continued down to her pussy and was pleased to find how wet she was.

He stood up with her in his arms and set her on her feet. Running his hand down the front of her body, he reached between them to play with her clit while suckling on her nipples. She moaned and fought halfheartedly to get away from him. He slid his other hand down her back to rest lightly on her derriere.

"Shit, Jean-Michel. Don't start something you can't finish."

He laughed. "You're standing close enough to me to know that I am more than able to finish what I'm starting. And you will always be fucked when I've finished punishing you."

She shook her head. "There's no way I can lie on my back or ride you."

He kissed her and smiled. "You will only be allowed to ride me as a special treat. You do not need to get any silly notions about your place in our bed. It will most always be beneath me or in front of me. The latter of which shouldn't prove too uncomfortable for you. Certainly less uncomfortable than I will be without easing my need for you." He led her back to their bed. "On your knees, Darby."

"Jean-Michel, no."

"Darby, yes. You are my mate and you will not fight me on my giving us both the pleasure and release we need that resulted from your foolishness. I said on your knees." He gave her a push toward the middle of the bed.

Darby crawled onto the bed on all fours. Jean-Michel got on the bed on his knees behind her and opened his fly. His now fully erect cock pointed right at her glistening pussy. He wasted no time in sinking balls deep into her warmth. As he made contact with her welted bottom she tried to move away. He grasped her hips and pulled her back.

"That hurts," she gasped.

"I'm sure it does," he soothed, "but that doesn't mean I'm not going to have you or that I will not make you call my name in your pleasure."

He began stroking her none too gently. He watched as she struggled between trying to move away from the contact he made with her welts when he surged forward and the pleasure she received as he did so. He moved within her and relished her response.

He stroked her hard and felt her pussy begin to contract around him. He groaned in response. Darby was incredibly responsive and he gloried in it. He could feel her begin to orgasm and stroked her harder. The strength of her climax caused her to crumple beneath him. It was only his grip on her pelvis and his cock buried deep within her that prevented her from totally collapsing. Without giving her any respite or chance to recover, he stroked her faster to bring her to another. He increased the frenzy of their coupling so that he could finish with her the second time she came calling his name. Then he withdrew from her and she fell onto her belly. Jean-Michel quickly stripped out of his clothes, sprawled on his back beside her, and pulled her to him.

He pushed her hair away from her face and tucked it behind her ears. He was surprised to see tears on her cheeks.

He leaned over her and wiped them away. "What troubles you, beloved?"

"Don't call me that."

"But you are my beloved, and you will see in time that I am yours. Talk to me, Darby. I would have us share all things."

"No," she said as she lay on her side, turning away from him.

He snuggled up behind her, careful now not to press too tightly against her welts. He draped one arm around her middle and held her close as he nuzzled her neck. "In time, beloved, you will turn toward me when you are in distress instead of away. Until then, I will hold you close so that you know I am here."

CHAPTER SEVEN

Jean-Michel held her close. Each time she tried to move away from his embrace, he pulled her back. The last time, he growled at her and simply said, "Enough." He felt her relax and finally settle into a deep sleep. Once assured she was truly asleep, he allowed himself to nuzzle her before holding her close and sleeping himself.

He woke once to make love to her, rolling her gently onto her back and ensuring her sore bottom was cradled on a soft pillow. There hadn't been a lot of foreplay as her body was more than ready to once again welcome him. He made sure she was aroused and ready and then gently mounted her, thrusting deep and causing her to climax as he did.

His lovemaking, while still dominating, was neither frenzied nor controlling. It was perhaps the most devastating of all. She clung to him and orgasmed repeatedly. He whispered what she assumed were assurances of love and devotion. She couldn't be sure because they were either in French, Cajun, or Creole… or some combination thereof. But they sounded sensual and hearing them increased her enjoyment.

As the sun came up, Darby awoke and realized that sometime during the night, Jean-Michel had rolled over on his back and tucked her in under his shoulder. One of his hands rested on the small of her back with his fingers just touching her ass. She started to pull away from him. His hand slipped down to cup her ass and gently pet her… a reminder that he was capable of putting additional sting in her tail if needed.

"Let go of me."

"Darby, do not start. The game is up, you revealed your true self to me the last time I made love to you." She said nothing. He chuckled. "Shall I remind you of your devotion to me?"

"I'm not devoted to you. I despise you."

His hand cracked down on her bottom.

"Bastard!"

"Mate," he corrected her. "And you will stop lobbing insults at me."

"If you don't want to be insulted, leave me the hell alone. And keep that thing away from me."

He laughed out loud. "That thing as you call it gave you immeasurable pleasure yesterday. You ought to be more appreciative."

"I don't appreciate having you wake me up to fuck me because you have a hard-on."

"I think, my mate, you need a little refresher in speaking more respectfully to me." He sat up on the edge of the bed and dragged her over his lap before she knew what he was about. He paddled her, reigniting the pain in her backside. "You are going to learn to speak respectfully even if you don't feel that way. Do you understand?"

He peppered her backside until she was squirming and thrashing about. He relit the painful fire on her backside, but the flame of her arousal blazed forth. His spankings were not only painful, they were humiliating. It was hard to reconcile the pain he was causing her with the resulting state of arousal.

"You sonofabitch!"

"Mate. Do you need to have your mouth washed out

again?"

"No," she cried.

He stopping spanking her and put his hand between her legs. She struggled to deny him access to her humiliation.

He chuckled, "As I suspected, you are wet and wanting."

He pulled her off his lap and stood up, tossing her on her belly over the end of the bed. He mounted her and began pummeling her pussy with his cock. Repeatedly his groin made contact with her very sore bottom and yet her pussy began to pulse in rhythm to his thrusting. Darby felt the beginning of her orgasm despite her trying to deny or stop it.

"Jean-Michel," she cried.

"Better, mate." He continued to thrust into her with considerable power and speed. "You, my beloved, are going to yield and call me mate before I'm through with you."

He settled into a rhythm that brought Darby to repetitive climaxes even though every time he surged forward into her, he came into direct and painful contact with her sore and welted backside. She couldn't get away from him—either literally or figuratively. Not only did he have a strong hold on her hips but she needed his strength and sexuality. She responded wildly to him.

"Who am I, Darby?"

"My captor."

He released her hip to swat her behind before taking hold of her again. "Who am I?"

"A sonofabitch," she cried. Again, he released her only long enough to land another swat on her bottom. "Jean-Michel, please."

"Please what, Darby?"

"Please come. I'm tired; I'm sore and I need you."

He slowed his stroking but continued to drive deep. "I know you do, beloved. Who am I?"

"Jean-Michel Gautier, alpha of New Orleans."

"Who am I to you?"

"No," she wailed.

"Yes, Darby. Who am I?"

"My mate," she cried as she climaxed again.

He pressed her down into the bed so that he could have more body contact with her. He increased the speed of his thrusting. "Yes, beloved. I am your mate. See that you don't forget it again." His last few words were said as he allowed himself to climax and spill himself deep within her.

He pulled out of her and pulled her into his lap and into his arms. She halfheartedly fought against him. He held her close and rained kisses across her face. "It's all right, beloved. I am your mate and you are mine. Everything will be fine."

"No, it won't."

He chuckled. "Yes, Darby, it will. Do you want to get ready and come downstairs with me or would you prefer to stay up here and I will have something sent up to you?"

"I can go downstairs?"

"You can, but you will be at my side at all times. If you misbehave, I will bring you back to our room, give you another spanking, and you will remain here for the rest of the day. Do you want to try coming downstairs?"

She nodded.

"Who are you?" he whispered. She looked at him and shook her head. He nuzzled her. "You can do this. Who are you?"

She sighed and felt silent tears run down her cheeks, only to be tenderly wiped away by Jean-Michel. "I am mate to the alpha of New Orleans."

"Yes, you are," he said, smiling. "But more precisely you are the beloved mate to the alpha of New Orleans. Now come, let's get showered and dressed."

• • • • • • •

Jean-Michel escorted Darby down the stairs, tucking her arm in his. They approached their hosts where Darby was informed about JD and Megan.

Dylan looked to Darby. "And how does the mistress of New Orleans fare this morning? I take it you have not been ill-used?"

"No more so than I have been since you destroyed our home and our pack."

"Darby," Skylar growled.

"Shh, *cariad*," said Dylan gently. "You know that the women of our pack speak freely as long as it is with a respectful tone. I assume your new mate disciplined you last night for your misbehavior yesterday? But it would appear he chose not to mark you at this time, and I daresay didn't knot and tie you to him?"

"No, but the bastard…"

"Not respectful, Darby," cautioned Dylan.

Jean-Michel hugged her close, infuriating her. "What she was going to say was but the bastard put her over his knee and spanked her pretty bottom until it was a deep shade of red and she chose to apologize for her behavior yesterday. Then when the same bastard put his hand between her legs and found her extremely wet and aroused for him, put her on her back on their bed and feasted on the honey he found there until she called for him to mount her and claim her pussy, which he did… repeatedly. That is what you meant to say, isn't it, sweetheart?"

"You prick," she seethed.

Jean-Michel gave her backside a hard swat. "Language, mate. We talked about that this morning. We agreed that you would be mindful of both the words you spoke and how you spoke them. Did we not?"

"I hate you."

"So you told me repeatedly this morning as I brought you to multiple orgasms. But as I recall, after a while you were far more interested in being stroked and pleasured than you were at lobbing insults in my direction. You, my naughty mate, are going to learn to behave if nowhere else than in public. Would you prefer to behave and remain downstairs or do you and I need to excuse ourselves so that you may have a further lesson in minding your mate?"

"No, Jean-Michel. I'll behave."

He pulled her into his arms and kissed her. She resisted at first, but then her mouth gave way and he deepened the kiss, leaving her breathless.

"Will you behave well enough to declare yourself in front of Dylan and Skylar?"

"Do I have a choice?"

"Of course you do… you always do. You can behave and do as I've asked or I can put you over my knee, give you a good spanking, and then you'll do it."

"Not much of a choice."

"I'm afraid it's the only one you have. Make it or I shall make it for you. I should tell you my choice will be the latter as my hand itches to spank your pretty bottom again and I grow hard at the thought of mounting you and hearing you call my name and promising to do as you're told."

The red on her cheeks deepened. Jean-Michel gathered Darby close and nuzzled her neck. He looked her directly in the eye and nodded with a questioning look. She nodded as well and he hugged her.

She turned to Skylar and Dylan. "I, Darby Callan, formerly of Bae Diogel, formally declare you, Jean-Michel Gautier, alpha of New Orleans to be my one true and lawful mate and alpha."

Jean-Michel let out a great howl before pulling her back into his embrace and kissing her thoroughly. "You have made me the happiest of men, mate. I will keep you happy, safe, and loved now and forever."

•••••••

Skylar and Dylan laid out various options with which people could enjoy themselves until dinner that evening. It was casual and nothing specific had been planned. The hope was that the remaining women from Bae Diogel would find men with whom they shared common interests.

Jean-Michel kept Darby within arm's reach at all times. At first, she had tried to remain aloof, but she was slowly but surely succumbing to his charm. A fact that annoyed her almost as much as it pleased him. He was attentive to her and made sure that whatever she wanted, with the exception of her freedom, was granted to her.

Megan spotted them and headed their way.

"Behave, Darby. Megan is happy to be with JD and to be joining our pack. Do not allow your own disquiet to take away from her joy in being mated to our beta."

"Whatever else you might think of me, you should know I would never want anything but happiness for a friend. Megan is my friend. She was my pack long before she was yours. If she's happy with him, then I'm happy for her. Unlike alpha males, those of us at Bae Diogel only want what is best for our friends and pack mates. Only we allow them to make the decision as to what constitutes best for them."

He chuckled and kissed her cheek. "Our pack is blessed to have a mistress who cares for those in her care… as am I."

"Bastard."

"Mate," he admonished as Megan greeted them both.

"Good morning, Jean-Michel. Darby?" Megan searched Darby's face to try to ascertain her well-being.

Darby made note of JD's mark on Megan. "Did you want that?" she asked quietly but loud enough so both JD and Jean-Michel heard her. Both growled low and menacingly.

"Yes, Darby. I did. JD called to me and unlike your obstinate, stubborn, and obnoxious self, I answered and without a lot of melodrama."

There was silence while the two male members of the New Orleans pack watched their mates with caution. Darby shrugged her shoulders. "Well, you always did have lousy taste in men."

There was an awkward silence, at least to Jean-Michel

and JD, until both women started laughing and embraced each other. Megan whispered in Darby's ear, "I'm so happy. Please let yourself be too."

Darby whispered back, "I'll try."

"I don't know, Jean-Michel, I think they may be conspiring against us."

Megan beamed at him. "Always, and we'll conscript all of the other women in our pack to rise up against you."

"Good thing we have far more men than women," laughed JD.

"Speak for yourself, *mon ami*," said Jean-Michel. "I have no need of help in seducing my mate into her rightful place beneath me, do I, mate?"

Darby shook her head but she was smiling. "Unfortunately, that is all too true."

"Do you understand even half of what he's saying to you when he fucks you? I swear I don't know what he's saying, but I like the sound of it anyway," giggled Megan.

Darby laughed. "I know. It bothered me the first few times. I've decided now, I don't really care what the words are, but I like how they make me feel."

"You will learn, my beloved. Just keep listening with your heart and you will come to know their meaning."

Darby looked at Jean-Michel and snorted. She turned to JD. "Does he always talk like this?"

JD laughed. "Only to those who have stolen his heart."

Darby and Megan both rolled their eyes as their mates laughed and hugged them close.

Jean-Michel watched as Megan coaxed Darby into feeling better about their future. Darby began to relax and laughed more easily. The two couples wandered down to the beach and walked with the two women in front followed by their mates.

"I think your Megan being with us will be good for my Darby."

"I believe you are right. But I think Darby would have settled with or without Megan. You may be too close to see it, but she already has softened to you. I believe our pack will be better with both of them as members. Do you think there's a chance we may be able to bring back one of the Bae Diogel girls who isn't already mated?" JD laughed as he said the last part.

Jean-Michel chuckled. "I know I'm going to try. I don't think any of the men we brought with us feels called to any of the remaining girls, but we have five unmated men at home. With or without another of the Bae Diogel girls, we need to start finding them mates."

JD nodded in agreement. "But that is a discussion for another day. For the rest of the day and evening, I plan to enjoy my new mate… and I would suggest, my friend, you do the same."

"That, *mon ami*, is an excellent suggestion."

•••••••

As the two couples headed back to the main house, Jean-Michel reached for Darby's hand and was delighted when she didn't pull it away. He brought it to his lips and kissed it before drawing her in for a kiss on her lips. JD and Megan watched them and then smiled at each other. They split up with JD and Megan heading down to the secondary residence in which they were staying and Jean-Michel and Darby heading up to the main house.

"You're not too terribly unhappy, are you, mate?"

Darby stopped and looked at him. She could see the concern on his face. "No. I suppose if I had to get auctioned off, you're not the worst one with whom I could end up."

Jean-Michel smiled at her. "And I feel I am the luckiest of men to have found my fated mate and made her mine."

Darby touched the mark left by her old mate. "But you haven't, have you… made me yours?"

Jean-Michel drew her close and said, "You are mine in every way that counts. You will always be mine. Never doubt that. I would eradicate his mark from your body as I would the bad memories you have of your time with him. But in time all will be as it should be."

"But what if I can never bear the thought of you forcing your knot into me…"

He laughed. "That will not last. You enjoy the pleasure I bring you far too much. Once you trust that I will never hurt you, you will be a greedy mate for my knot."

"Look, Jean-Michel, I really do understand how kind you've been… the five welts I have on my ass notwithstanding. I just wish there was something I could give you to let you know that without feeling I've capitulated completely or…"

"How about a small concession… say a promise that you will behave yourself until midnight."

She giggled. "Uhm, I don't know, that's an awfully long time… unless, of course, you plan to take me back to your bed."

He smiled. "Our bed, beloved. I think my mate is finding pleasure in my arms, *n'est pas?*"

"I could say no just to be difficult, but we'd both know I was lying."

"Yes, we would. So, are you willing to give me your word?"

"Yes. I will not try to escape or shorten your life and in general will behave until at least midnight… provided part of that time is spent with you in bed."

He laughed out loud. "If all it takes to make you behave is spending great amounts of time daily with me in our bed, then you shall be the best behaved mate of all."

She giggled again. "I see Skylar. Would you mind if I went and talked with her for a moment?"

"Not at all. But keep in mind that I expect you to be pleasant and respectful to our hostess."

Darby kissed him and headed toward Skylar.

As she approached, Skylar greeted her. "Hey, Dar. How are you? I don't think I've seen you at all today without Jean-Michel in close attendance."

"This morning I refused to give him my word that I wouldn't try to bolt at the earliest moment, but once I gave him my word I would behave at least until midnight he seems to have relaxed."

"Midnight? Afraid his carriage will turn back into a pumpkin?"

"I'm no Cinderella and he sure as hell isn't Prince Charming."

Skylar raised her eyebrow in question.

"Okay, so maybe he's pretty damned charming."

They both laughed and then Darby turned sober. "I don't have a choice, do I?"

"The only choice any of us have is whether or not to be happy. Jean-Michel is your fated mate. You heard him call to you. You know that."

"I don't want a fated mate."

"Neither did Roz, and I didn't want another one, but here we are."

"One thing he's got going for him is he's pretty great in the sack."

Skylar laughed. "At one point he told Dylan that no woman had ever refused his knot or not found happiness in his bed."

"That sounds like him. Although he hasn't pushed the whole knot thing." A dark shadow crossed her face. "That won't last, will it?"

"No. Nor will the not marking you. I think he's trying to be understanding and considerate of your feelings, but that mark has got to bother him tremendously and not being able to knot you is painful. Do you have bad experiences with being knotted and tied?"

"Nothing like Lacey, but not good." She touched the mark from her former mate. "He wasn't overly considerate about forcing that thing inside me. Some of the time he let me catch my breath long enough to relax and accommodate it, but then some short jabs and it would feel like he just gushed into me. But once he was done dumping his load in me, he was done and he'd yank that thing back out."

"That's not what it's supposed to be like. They do need to give you time to adjust to the knot and then in order to avoid hurting you or themselves they need to wait until it goes down."

"How long does that take?"

"In human form anywhere from one to three hours. In wolf? Thirty to forty-five minutes."

"Is it every time they fuck you?"

"Not usually. But it can, if it's pleasurable for both of you, be a couple of times a week, but at least monthly. I really think you could be happy with him if you gave it a chance."

"Meg thinks so too. But then she's gone daffy on JD and he is nuts about her. She tells me it's because she yielded to his call as his mate."

"She's right. Dylan is hoping all of you will be called… and that all of you will answer," she said pointedly.

"All right, so I heard him. God damn alpha roll and that call knocked me off my feet, literally. And I thought that SOB beta of yours had a hard hand. Christ, when Jean-Michel connects with my ass, it hurts like there's no tomorrow. But damn, he makes up for it afterward. I swear he knows just how to get me where he wants me."

Skylar nodded. "I think it comes with the fated mate thing. Dylan has a power over my body and my responses that are amazing."

"What's he going to do about the rest of them?"

"He's trying to figure that out. He's talked to not just the men, but to our women as well. If you can, encourage them to talk to him or me."

Skylar saw Darby shiver. "You'll get used to that… and they can feel your presence as well."

"Which, my beloved," said Jean-Michel, coming up behind her, "means I will always be able to find you. In addition to being able to detect your life sign, I always have your scent in my nostrils. So, run if you must, but I will run you down. And remember that your first spanking was for running from Dylan, not from me. I will not be as lenient should you choose to test me again."

"You had to threaten me. Here I was thinking maybe you weren't so bad."

"Not a threat, mate. A promise. You are the one who refuses to yield, to accept my mark and ask me to knot and tie you. Instead you threaten to leave me and/or to shorten my life." He took her face in his hands and kissed her. "But you will come around, mate, and we will be deliriously happy."

"You're already delirious. How about if I offer to extend the deadline on not trying to leave and actually trying to behave until after dinner tomorrow?"

He kissed her again. "That would make me very happy. Is that what you're doing?"

She nodded. "I know I haven't been very accepting of all of this and I do know it's an honor to be mated to you…"

He pulled her close and rubbed her back to comfort her. "I know, beloved. I know how hard it's been, but 'twill get better. I think we'd best head upstairs so you can change for dinner."

Skylar looked around. "Dinner isn't for hours."

"Perhaps, but I'd like to take advantage of my mate's largess and lure her back into our bed."

Darby laughed at him. "You've had worse ideas, mate."

Jean-Michel looked over her head at Skylar. He tried not to overreact to Darby calling him mate for the first time.

CHAPTER EIGHT

Darby preceded Jean-Michel up the stairs but held his hand. When they got to the top of the stairs, she waited until he too was on the landing and then offered her mouth to his. Never one to pass on an invitation, he captured her mouth and leisurely explored it as he held her close.

"Take me," she whispered.

Jean-Michel smiled. Darby liked how his smile changed his whole face. In repose or anger, it was strong and angular. His eyes were a dark, seemingly bottomless pool of deep brown. But when aroused or highly amused, they took on an almost golden glow. His face became softer, still very masculine, but more open and inviting.

"With pleasure, mate." He opened the door to their room and ushered her in before him. As he closed the door he wrapped his arm around her middle and pulled her back into his chest. When he felt no resistance at all, he smiled and began kissing her neck and down the top of her shoulders.

Darby leaned back into him and brought the hand not wrapped around her middle up to fondle her breast. She made a low growl of frustration when he removed it. That caused him to swat her hard. But before she could react to that, he ran his hand up under her sweater and pushed her bra up over her breast so he could have his hands on her flesh and take her hardening nipple in his fingers. Darby relaxed back against him and sighed contentedly.

Jean-Michel chuckled low and nuzzled her neck. He splayed out the hand with which he'd been holding her and slid it down her body, opening the fly of her jeans and running his hand between her legs. He rubbed her clit with the ball of his thumb, causing her to squirm against him. She tried to pull away but he held her close both with the hand between her legs and the one that was fondling her breast.

"Do not think to pull away from me, mate. You are mine."

"Yes, Jean-Michel."

She snuggled back against him and he enjoyed her lack of argument. His mate could be most agreeable when she tried. "What do you want, mate?" He held his breath to see what her answer might be.

"You. I want you."

He released her and turned her to face him. "That, beloved, you already have. Shall I take you to bed and spend the afternoon between your legs?"

"Yes, please," she said, smiling seductively.

He pulled her sweater over her head and unhooked her bra. Her breasts fell free and he dipped his head to take one in his mouth, sucking hard. He slid his hands down her back and over her buttocks, being careful not to apply too much pressure but sliding her jeans down. It occurred to him that she had not put on any panties before they went downstairs. The realization made him have to focus a bit more on suppressing the knot that threatened to form.

"Naughty mate."

"What, for not wearing panties? They were very uncomfortable on those welts you gave me. Besides, no one could tell."

"A reasonable reason not to have them on, but you should have told me."

She giggled and wrapped her arms around his neck, rubbing her tits against his chest. "And does my mate like the idea of me without panties on?"

"Very much. But from now on, you ask permission to do so. I would find it very distracting to know you were without panties and there for the taking."

She giggled again. She reached between them and began to unbutton his shirt. He allowed her to pull it off of him. She took hold of his belt and he stilled her hand. "You ask first," he said.

"Yes, Jean-Michel. Please, mate, might I unbuckle your belt so I can open your fly and get your cock out?"

He laughed. She unbuckled the belt and opened his fly. His cock immediately rose up and out so that she was confronted with it. "It seems I wasn't the only one going commando," she said.

"No, but my reason was so if I had a chance to fuck you, I had less to get in the way." He shucked off his jeans and swept her up in his arms, carrying her to their bed. "And now that we're both naked, there is nothing to keep me from ravaging you for the rest of the afternoon."

"You do realize I still have a sore ass from the spankings you gave me as well as you repeatedly fucking me, don't you?"

"Are you complaining?"

"About the latter, no. I could have skipped the spanking part, especially with that nasty belt."

"I will only use my belt if it is warranted. Trying to run from me and doing so in a manner that could have caused you great harm warrants it. I would tell you that you could avoid being spanked if you behaved, but we both know you aren't capable of that. So, I'll just tell you that I'll never spank you harder than I love you afterward. Can you agree to that?"

She nodded. "And I suppose if I tried to tell you that I didn't get aroused from you spanking me that would constitute a lie and I'd get spanked again for that."

"And have your mouth washed out with soap." He laid her on the bed and lay down next to her. "God, you're beautiful." He ran his nose down the length of her body from her lips on her face to the lips between her legs, breathing deeply. "You smell of the ocean and crepe jasmine. Do you know that all of the Gautier mates who came before you smell of crepe jasmine? It is unique to our pack and part of how we know you are one of us."

She reached between them and wrapped her hand around his cock. It was hard and warm to her touch. She squeezed him gently and stroked him lightly. She heard a grumbling noise from deep within his throat. Not really a growl but not quite a purr. "Does my mate like it when I hold him in my hand?"

He grinned at her. His cock was now throbbing and it took every ounce of self-control not to allow the knot to form, roll her to her back, and force it past her opening. "Your mate is not in the mood nor can he stand much of your playing." He pushed her over onto her back and pinned her beneath him as he began to kiss her.

His hand moved from rolling her nipple between his thumb and forefinger down to do the same thing with her clit and then moved back up to her nipple. She moaned and writhed under his attention. He began to kiss his way down her body. He suckled both of her nipples, going back and forth between the two.

"Jean-Michel, please?"

He chuckled in a highly sensual and possessive way. He had her body responding to his ministrations in just the way he wanted. She tried in vain to stay underneath him. It was obvious to him that she would far rather he parted his thighs with his own and mounted her. However, he meant to savor her wild honey. He wanted her so primed and ready that she came as he drove his cock home into her.

He nuzzled her as he worked his way down her body, alternating licking and tasting her with kisses. When he moved down to get between her legs she parted them easily and he was greeted with an abundance of her to taste. He swirled his tongue around her clit and she bowed her body, driving her pussy up and into his face as she came.

He chuckled again at her response and then set about arousing and getting her to the point of climax so that when he mounted her, he would sink into her as she contracted around him in orgasm. He nibbled her lower lips and licked the outer rim of her opening. She squirmed and writhed as he lapped up her honey. He plunged his tongue into her to lap more deeply.

"God, Jean-Michel."

He reared his head and upper body and watched her. "Does my beloved wish to be mounted and finished by her mate?"

"Yes, please?"

He moved up her body until he was poised over her, his cock hard and throbbing. "Open your eyes, Darby. I want you to look at me when I mount you."

She opened her eyes and fell into his. She could feel the last remnants of her will to resist him and his call fade away. "I see you," she whispered. She wound her arms around him, pulling him to her.

"Do you, beloved?"

"Yes. I yield to my mate and alpha. Claim me."

He lowered himself as he moved up.

She could not hold his gaze and closed her eyes.

"No, beloved. See me."

She did and climaxed as his cock breached her opening and he drove home. He moved in her strongly and wrapped her in his arms. He stroked her hard and she responded. As she began to climb toward her own peak again, he felt his canines elongate.

Her eyes never left his as he opened his mouth and lowered his head. His mouth covered the mark of her former mate.

"Now, please," she whispered.

He sank his teeth into her and heard her gasp of pain.

He knew later he would tend to her to ease the pain he needed to cause her. But he would not stop before he had removed the repulsive evidence of the man who had claimed her before and abused her.

He shook her as gently as he could, feeling the old mark give way and the spot meant for him and him alone accept his marking. He drove into her as he marked her. Her pussy convulsed in response to his plunging cock. He used his strong thighs and buttocks to drive deeply into her core. He felt her orgasm beneath him as he thrust repeatedly into her pussy and began to release his cum into her. Having finally marked her as his, he began to kiss the deep wound and nuzzled her, whispering to her in words she didn't comprehend but in a language she understood.

He raised his head and looked into her beautiful blue eyes. He saw no recrimination or fear, only his love for her being reflected back at him. He started to speak and she put her hand over his mouth to stay his tongue.

"Is it gone?" She didn't remove her hand.

He nodded.

"And your mark will be the only thing that shows?"

Again, he nodded, never losing eye contact with her.

"I'm yours? No one can take me away from you?"

He removed her hand. "You have always been mine, beloved. Nothing but death will part us. And death to anyone who tries or causes you harm," he vowed.

He slowly pulled out of her and rolled to his side, bringing her with him. She snuggled next to him of her own accord. They slept briefly but she was awakened when she heard the door to the closet in their room close. "What are you doing?"

"Shh. I want to get a cloth to clean your mark. I want to ensure I didn't bite you too deep."

She beckoned him back with her hand. "Come back to bed. I'm fine."

He returned to her, kissed her deeply, and then walked into the bath. He came back out with a warm cloth and pressed it against the wound to stop the bleeding and gently cleaned around it. Her wolf nature allowed it to start healing, but it would leave a bold scar representing his claiming her.

She reached up, pushed his long hair out of his face, and tucked it behind his ear. He smiled, caught her hand, and kissed her fingertips. He too brushed her hair out of her eyes. He leaned down and touched his lips very lightly to the mark.

He left her briefly to put the cloth away and walked toward the bed. She pulled back the covers, revealing her naked body. He slid in next to her and she nestled against him. They wrapped their arms around each other and fell back asleep.

Sometime later she whispered, "Jean-Michel? Are you awake?"

He opened his eyes and smiled at her. "What would you have me say, mate? No?"

She giggled. "No, but do you mind me waking you?"

"No, sweetheart. If you have need of me, you must always wake me. What do you require?"

She sat up, looking down at him, her breasts at eye level with her nipples fully aroused. "I want you to see me."

"I always see you… even with my eyes closed." He reached up and lazily traced the outline of her areola before rubbing his thumb across her nipple, causing her to moan.

"I wanted you to see me behaving."

He laughed at her. "Afraid it won't happen very often so I should be sure to make note when it does?"

"Yes. Because all I want to do is throw my leg over you and lower myself onto that gorgeous cock of yours, but you told me that I only got to ride you as a special treat. I think marking me should be considered a special occasion and I should get a treat."

"Do you? And here I thought giving you my mark was special enough." He saw doubt enter her eyes. "I'm teasing you, Darby. You gifted me by agreeing to be marked by me."

Darby grinned and pinned him down beneath her and then moved to throw her leg over him. She wasn't quite sure how he had done it, but she suddenly found herself on her back with her mate between her legs driving his hard cock up into her waiting sheath. She felt her body move up to join with his and she gloried in his strong embrace and vigorous lovemaking. As she had come to expect, her whole body came alight with need for him. She had never known she had the capacity for multiple orgasms. With Jean-Michel she found that he demanded her body respond to him repeatedly. He enjoyed the feeling her orgasms provided him and wanted to ensure that he pleasured her to the point of exhaustion before he allowed himself the ultimate pleasure of his release. She came twice before he took hold of her hips, no longer allowing her to move as he drove into her repeatedly before he spilled himself in her. He collapsed on her.

"Jean-Michel?"

"You must give me a little time to recover, my greedy mate."

She giggled. "Really? Kind of feels like you're doing that already. But I was going to point out to you that if we're going to make dinner, we probably need to get showered and dressed."

"Yes, dinner is to be formal tonight.'

She frowned. "I have nothing to wear that's suitable for a formal occasion."

"You have not checked the closet. You could outshine all of the women here in a pair of sweatpants and one of my shirts, but I thought you might like something more befitting your position as mistress of the New Orleans pack. There are two dresses in the closet for you. Choose whichever you like."

He got up and helped her up. They took a shower together and came back into the room. Darby opened the closet and gasped. There before her were two of the most beautiful cocktail dresses she'd ever seen. They were both of a brilliant cobalt blue. One was a high-necked halter with a low open back. The other had an asymmetrical neckline that formed an opening over the spot where he had removed her former alpha's mark and replaced it with his own. One would hide his mark and the other show it off.

"Jean-Michel, they're beautiful, but too much."

"Too much what?" he said, grinning at her.

"Too expensive. I don't need anything like this."

He laughed and kissed her. "My darling Darby. You are mate to the alpha of New Orleans, one of the oldest and wealthiest packs on Earth. We have holdings and income from all over the world. If you want a closet full of designer dresses, shoes, and handbags, they are yours."

She looked at him in astonishment. "You mean… we're rich?" she whispered.

He laughed again. "Filthy." He was almost finished putting his clothes on. "Now go put one of the dresses on and let's go join JD, Megan, and the rest of those gathered here."

"Which would you like to see me in?"

"I like seeing you naked…"

"Oh, really?" she teased.

"But only for me. Bianca couldn't decide between them so I told her to get both. You choose."

Darby had to fight back tears as she realized that while both dresses were beautiful, one would cover the area that showed her mark and the other would ensure that all eyes were riveted to the spot. She knew without a doubt which she wanted to wear.

She walked out of the bathroom and saw his face light up. "You are, my mate, truly stunning. But if you prefer the other, do not feel you have to wear this one to soothe my ego."

She laughed. "I'm not, but I love the fact that you gave me the choice. I hated his mark. Every time I touched it, I recoiled not only from the mark itself but from the memory and what it represented. This," she said, touching it lightly,

"I choose to show to the world and declare that I am the one true and lawful mate to the alpha of New Orleans."

He kissed her deeply and, looking into her eyes, said, "That you are, my beloved. And I am your one and true lawful mate, and grateful and humbled to be so."

CHAPTER NINE

JD and Megan entered the room arm in arm. Megan looked happy and relaxed with her mate. The juncture of her throat and collarbone showed faint traces of the mark JD had made when he'd claimed her. It was only the mark of an alpha that took time to heal and left a scar that never faded.

Jean-Michel and Darby followed them. Darby's body language indicated her mate had been successful in luring her back to their bed. Darby's dress was cobalt blue and emphasized her eyes. She seemed to be scanning the room. When her eyes alighted on Skylar she smiled broadly and then turned to Jean-Michel.

Darby reached up to whisper something in Jean-Michel's ear and nuzzle his neck. He ran his hand possessively down her flank and kissed her but allowed her to leave his side. As she turned toward Skylar the two women smiled at each other. Darby was certain Skylar could see the fresh mark from Jean-Michel.

"He's watching me, isn't he?" Darby asked Skylar as she got close.

"Yes, but not in the way a man watches someone he's worried about bolting, but rather that of a well-sated and happy mate."

"I know he's the former and he'd better be the latter."

Skylar looked at Jean-Michel again, whose very essence spoke to his joy in his new mate and in her accepting his mark. "Oh, he is. I've rarely seen a man look so happy with himself… or his mate." She nodded her head toward the fresh mark. "Are you all right with that?"

"Surprisingly, yes. Do you know he made sure that they got me two party dresses—one that showed it off and one which covered it. He wanted me to make the choice about whether or not to show it. Jesus, I'd forgotten how much that hurts."

Skylar smiled. "I know. I do think Dylan's hurt more than Micah's. I suspect they have to bite deeper and harder in order to eradicate your former mate's marking."

"Were you okay with his doing that? Getting rid of Micah's mark?"

"Other than how much it hurt, I understand it. Alphas are notoriously possessive and territorial. Seeing the mark that jackass that you were mated to before had to be difficult for him. He'd want to rid you of that mark not only to place his own there, but also to wipe away that last vestige of your former mate. The need to mark their mates as their own is overwhelming for an alpha."

Darby nodded. "In many ways, I think the need to eradicate that jackass' mark from my body was even more compelling than marking me with his own. Do you know he offered to kill my former mate for me?"

"Yes. He told me you turned him down but asked if I thought that's what you really wanted. I have no doubt if he thought it would bring you any peace or lessen the memories of what you suffered, he'd kill him and feed him to the alligators."

Darby laughed. "I think you're right. I have to say that every time he fucks… no, that isn't what he does. He makes love to me. Can you believe it, Sky? I can actually say that and believe it. Every time he makes love to me, the shit I lived through with that jerk lessens. More and more, it's like I started to live the other day when he claimed me."

"Funny how you can find the relationship of a lifetime that starts with a spanking."

"I know, what the hell is up with that? He has wicked hands when he's pissed and expressing his displeasure with my behavior on my ass. But those same hands can make me climax more than once before he even mounts me." She turned to look at him and he smiled at her. "Gods, he's gorgeous, isn't he?"

Skylar nodded.

"And he's all mine. He is, isn't he?"

"Absolutely. When an alpha takes a fated mate, he really loses any and all sexual interest in other women. And no man who looks at you the way he does would have eyes for anyone else."

"So, he looks at me the way Dylan looks at you? You are happy, aren't you, Sky?"

"Yes, more than I should be. And I'm coming to find, as I'm sure you are, that they're cut from a different cloth than the old guard. They genuinely care for the women in their care."

"I know. Jean-Michel said that Dylan has taken a lot of shit over the way he's handled this. My mate admires your mate a great deal."

Skylar smiled. "There's a lot to admire."

"As much as he wants to, Jean-Michel thinks he should wait until we're home to knot me. He wants me in our bed where he can ensure that I'm pampered and cared for… a bit of a difference from what I was used to. Thing is, I'm actually starting to want him to… to knot me, that is. He confirmed what you said the other night that if done correctly, it is deeply intimate and sensual and like nothing I've ever done."

Skylar laughed. "Well, let me put it to you this way… Roz was downright pissed I'd never told her how incredible it was after Oliver knotted her for the first time."

Darby laughed. "That sounds like Roz. Do you think she'll be all right up in the Hamptons?"

"You didn't get to see much of them together. I think she'll be fine anywhere she's with Oliver. I'm starting to believe we may all come out of this in good shape. Dylan has said we won't lose touch and if any of our women are abused, the abuser will answer to him."

"If he's anything like his beta, that could get ugly."

"Anyone who isn't me should be considered ugly by you, my love," said Jean-Michel as he swiftly closed the distance between them and wrapped his arms around his mate.

"Ugly, stupid, and lousy in bed," replied Darby, causing Jean-Michel to laugh and kiss her neck just above his mark. "Quit fretting," she said quietly as she stroked the side of his face. "It really doesn't bother me."

"Careful, mate, lying to me even to soothe my feelings is a spankable offense, *n'est pas*?"

"It's not really a lie. Was it painful and does it hurt? Yes, but I knew it would be when I asked you to do it. The fact that you waited until I asked and have been so loving to me makes the pain negligible. I don't think that rises to the level of lying to you."

"That is all true. But when I ask you if something hurts, I want you to answer me without regard for my feelings. The only other woman you know of our pack is Megan and she hasn't been home yet either. But like with Dylan's pack, the women in our pack know they may speak their minds if done respectfully."

"Well, then, with all due respect… you didn't ask me if it hurt. I could just tell you were fretting again."

Jean-Michel laughed. "Point taken, my love." He looked to Skylar. "Tell me, are all the women of Bae Diogel this difficult to deal with and so easy to love?"

"I'm afraid so," said Dylan, joining them. "Frightfully easy to love. I find they are much easier to deal with when marked and then spanked and knotted on a regular basis, eh, *cariad*? I see your mate bears your mark."

Jean-Michel nodded. "Yes, *mon ami*, at her request. She no longer bears the mark of that bastard that abused her, but instead has that of the man whose heart and soul are in her keeping."

Dylan smiled. "I think we're getting ready to go into dinner. Would the two of you mind joining the ranking members of my pack in my study after dinner? And have JD and Megan join us if you don't mind."

Jean-Michel nodded and then followed with Darby as Dylan announced dinner and then led Skylar into the dining room.

•••••••

The dinner was a grand success. All of those gathered around the table seemed to be enjoying themselves. Jean-Michel was honored that Dylan had asked him to sit at the other end of his table. He was even more honored to have Darby at his side, resplendent in her new dress and proudly bearing his mark.

As dinner broke up, Jean-Michel, Darby, JD, and Megan joined the ranking members of Calon Gwyllt in Dylan's study. Their discussion centered around the three remaining members of Bae Diogel who were not mated—Summer, Gina, and Lacey. All in attendance agreed that Summer was the most problematic, mostly because she had no desire to be happy.

There was a knock on the door and Lacey and the alpha from Savannah, Beau Butler, asked to speak with Dylan. They were not opposed to the others remaining. Beau had come to ask to be able to claim Lacey as his mate. Jean-Michel smiled as he watched Dylan ensure this was what Lacey wanted as well. Beau affectionately chided his mate for trying to hide from him.

"This seems to be a common occurrence in the women of your pack, beloved," Jean-Michel whispered to Darby. Darby's affectionate elbow to his ribs was answered by an affectionate swat to her behind. The difference being that Jean-Michel did not have bruised ribs, while Darby's bottom was still smarting from Jean-Michel's previous punishments.

The young couple was congratulated and left the study after Beau pledged to support Dylan if ever the need arose. Jean-Michel feared that the need would arise, and not in the too distant future.

Jean-Michel spoke up. "At the risk of being a greedy bastard, which of course, I am…" and everyone laughed. "We could easily settle the question of Summer."

"Easily?" asked Nick. "There is nothing easy about Summer. She's dead set on being unhappy and running away again."

"What's your thinking, Jean-Michel?" asked Dylan.

"Send Summer home with us. I know, I know, but really, are they going to be more pissed that I managed to convince you to trust me with three as opposed to two? I have seven unmated males in my pack and no unmated females. Summer could be happy with us. She would have Meg and my beautiful Darby to help her. I think she needs more time to adjust and to decide to be happy… and I don't think that's time you can give her."

"You'd really want to take her on?" asked Dylan. Jean-Michel nodded.

After additional discussion, Dylan seemed to settle on the idea of sending Summer to New Orleans. He cautioned Jean-Michel that his pack might find itself under attack.

Jean-Michel laughed and said, "Let them come. We could use the exercise."

•••••••

The group adjourned until the following morning. Summer was to be invited to join all of the guests for brunch and afterward, a decision would be made about with whom to send Gina.

Jean-Michel and Darby headed back upstairs and entered their room. Once inside Darby turned and embraced the man she now called mate and alpha, pressing her body against his and covering his mouth with her own.

He chuckled as she pushed her tongue past his lips and teeth to taste and explore as he so often did to her. He wrapped his arms around her and held her close, savoring her need to be with him. He had to focus to keep the knot from forming. Every instinct from this moment back a millennium or more urged him to let the knot form, seat himself deep within her and allow the knot to swell, sealing her to him. But tomorrow would be a taxing day at best for her and he wanted to minimize any discomfort she might have on the trip home.

Darby could feel his cock getting hard and the beginnings of a knot. "Are you going to knot and tie me to you this night, mate?"

He smiled and kissed her lightly. Searching her face, he knew that she would not protest if he allowed the knot to form and possessed her completely.

"It pleases me to know that you no longer fear the time when I will knot and tie you. But like when you first lost your virginity, it may be painful, not just from the knot itself, but from the entire act. I would prefer that we were at home."

"Is it that painful?" she asked, no longer afraid but wanting to understand what to expect.

"It can be when I first force it inside you. But as responsive and sensual as you are, mate, once I have you sealed to me and begin to rock you, I have no doubt that all you will think about when you feel a knot starting to form is arousal and joy knowing it will be yours that night."

She giggled. "That sure of yourself, are you?"

"No, beloved, that sure of you and your response to my lovemaking. But you will most likely be sore. I want you to be able to rest comfortably so that when I knot and tie you repeatedly over the next several days, you will be able to enjoy the experience."

She smiled seductively. "But what if I want it now, tonight?"

He chuckled and tapped her nose with his finger. "As much as I love you, you will not always get what you want when you want it and when you misbehave because of it, you will get your pretty bottom spanked. I would suggest that you avoid that as well before we make our way home."

"How far are we from New Orleans? And do we live in the city proper?"

"We are about three hours by plane and more than sixteen by car."

"How many times do we have to change planes?"

"None. We have a private jet."

"We have a private jet? Jesus, you really are rich."

"We, my beloved, and our pack is very wealthy. We have accumulated and protected our wealth for hundreds of years. It helps that Jean Laffite was an excellent privateer and invested heavily as he became successful. So, we started with a sizeable fortune and each generation has added to that wealth and financial security."

"But a jet?"

"A small one. It will only hold ten people."

"Oh, only ten? Well, I'd better tell Dylan I need someone with more money," she said, giggling as she turned from him and started toward their bed.

His hand connected with her backside. "That, mate, is not funny," but he was smiling as he said it and the swat had little power behind it. "And in the future, you could earn a trip over my knee for saying something like that."

She turned around and wrapped her arms back around him. "But it is funny. For you see, as much as you would kill anyone who tried to take me from you? I would do the same. I'm afraid you're stuck with me until the end of time."

He threw back his head and laughed. "It will probably take me at least that long to teach you to be well behaved. Now, mate, you have on entirely too many clothes."

To Darby's delight it didn't take him long to divest both of them of their clothing and take her to bed. As much as he had enjoyed making her respond to him when she didn't choose to, his joy in her happiness in being in his embrace was greater than any he had ever experienced before.

When finally he let her rest and was sprawled on his back with her tucked under his shoulder, she said to him, "Jean-Michel? Tell me about your…"

"Our," he corrected gently.

She smiled. "…our home. Do we live in the city itself like in the French Quarter or… oh lord, the only things I know about New Orleans are the French Quarter, Bourbon Street, beignets, and Mardi Gras."

"We keep a large Creole-style townhome in the French Quarter itself. It has four bedrooms and three and a half baths, a full basement, and a kitchen that was designed for entertaining. We have a large courtyard off of the back with greenery and a lovely fountain. When we entertain business guests not of our kind, we most often will do it there. It is also used by pack members when they want to be in the city for various functions including Mardi Gras. But like most of the larger, more affluent packs, we have a large estate in what is known as Plantation County about an hour from the heart of the Crescent City."

"Did we grow cotton and have slaves?"

"No. We grew indigo, sugar, and other crops. The Gautiers have never owned slaves, which didn't always make us very popular with other plantation owners. In fact, both the townhouse and the estate were utilized by the Underground Railroad to help runaway slaves."

"I like that we didn't own slaves and helped those who managed to get away to get to safety."

"And I like that you are beginning to understand you are a Gautier and ours is a rich heritage."

"Do we have just one huge house or several big houses?"

"We are set up much like Dylan's estate. We have three large residences and then several small dwellings. The main house is for the ranking members of the pack."

"I've met JD. Megan is mad about him, you know."

Jean-Michel nodded.

"Who is our omega? Does he have a mate?"

"That would be Geoff and no, he does not. Part of me hopes that Summer is his mate, and part does not."

"Why? Do you think the Ruling Council would throw a fit if all three of the ranking members of our pack were mated to those rogues from Bae Diogel?"

"Would you like it if they objected?"

"I wouldn't want it to cause actual trouble for us. But if it caused them to lose sleep, then yes, I would."

He laughed. "I couldn't care less what they think. And if they choose to bring trouble to our door, we will cure them of their arrogance in thinking they can dictate to a member pack."

"Then, why do you care?"

"I want to ensure that our unmated males know I am committed to finding them mates and didn't snag the most amazing women for ranked members only. I also worry that she might not be the best choice for the wife of our omega. It is always best if the mate to the omega has those tendencies as well."

"You haven't seen Summer at her best…"

"I've barely seen Summer at all as she has been so naughty that she has spent most of her time upstairs in her room, which I'm beginning to wonder wasn't what she wanted all along."

"She's really very nice. Please don't judge her just based on your limited interaction with her. If you'd only judged me on my behavior, I wouldn't be lying here naked next to you."

"Yes, but then I was called to you and you to me. Although, naughty mate that you are, you resisted my call."

"At the risk of supporting your already inflated ego, that wasn't easy. When I heard you howl, I could feel it reverberate through my bones. When you got closer, it spread like wildfire through my blood. Combined with that alpha roll you sent at me, I never had a chance. That really wasn't fair."

"All is fair in love and war. And with you, beloved, it was both."

"I know, I really was awful. I'm so sorry."

"No need, *ma choue*. Our family has a long and storied history of difficult mates. We know that the more they resist, the sweeter their surrender will be. And yours was the sweetest of all."

CHAPTER TEN

The following morning the guests began to gather around the dining room. It was a casual and relaxed gathering and everyone looked forward to seeing what marvels Thomas had created for their culinary enjoyment.

Summer had once again joined the group and took no time in proving how unrelenting she could be in not wanting to be happy. Both Dylan and Nick admonished her more than once. Having had his fill and making his decision about her fate, Dylan asked Nick to remove her to his study to try to talk some sense into her. But that having done no good, Nick once again escorted her to her room and put a man on guard outside her door. He found JD and the two of them sought out the alphas of their respective packs.

As they walked, JD offered, "Let's get Jean-Michel. If she's coming home with us, she may as well get used to the idea that she'll get disciplined by either Jean-Michel or myself."

Nick laughed. "You're welcome to her. I'd like to spend one day of this house party enjoying myself rather than having to chase down and/or discipline some member of Bae Diogel. They are difficult," he said as they found Jean-Michel and Dylan standing together.

Having overheard him, Jean-Michel laughed. "Not difficult, Nick, spirited. I take it our Summer has once again been sent to her room?" He turned to Dylan. "If you're going to send her home with us, I'd just as soon introduce her to discipline New Orleans style."

Dylan nodded. "She may as well start answering to you as her alpha. I'm giving Summer over to your care, Jean-Michel."

"We will do right by her, Dylan. Please assure your mate she is in good hands. JD, please place one of our men on her door and inform the lady I will see to her myself after brunch."

JD nodded toward one of the men from the New Orleans pack and took him to the other residence where Summer had been staying.

As JD entered the room, Summer said, "Who the hell are you?"

"I'm JD of the New Orleans pack and your beta. Best have a care as to how you speak with me, little girl."

"Roz Kincanon was my beta. Now, I recognize no person as such."

"Whether or not you recognize me as such does not change the fact that I am. Dylan has entrusted your care and well-being to our alpha, Jean-Michel. As this will be your first punishment within our pack, he will see to it himself. I urge you to lose your surly, petulant attitude. It will not serve you well with him."

"Fuck off."

JD laughed. "I'd best let Mrs. Hastings know we'll be needing to buy more goat's milk soap. I have a feeling we're going to need it. Jean-Michel will be up to see to your correction in a bit. Were I you, I'd be either standing in the corner or sitting on this bed with a very contrite expression."

"Good thing you're not me."

JD laughed again. "Yes. I would not want to have our alpha angry or disappointed in my behavior. We'll see how long that haughtiness lasts once he puts you over his knee. My guess is that it won't be long." JD left her.

•••••••

Jean-Michel waited until JD had returned and they had been able to enjoy the sumptuous brunch. He informed Darby that her friend was about to get a taste of her new alpha's discipline. As he thought it might, it upset her. He soothed her and reminded her that she did not get to make the decision about when and how females in their pack were punished. But that he did see her role as being supportive of them afterward without encouraging further bad behavior. He rose to head to the other house and go up to Summer. He asked that JD see to having their people start gathering their things to take out to the plane. Darby again tried to advocate on Summer's behalf.

"She's just so unhappy and scared. The raid really rattled her and everything has been in upheaval ever since. Please don't be harsh with her, Jean-Michel," Darby pleaded for her friend.

He bent down and kissed the top of her head. "Enough, Darby. You have pleaded her case. And if this was the first display of this behavior from her, I might be inclined to be lenient. But as you pointed out, I don't know Summer at all… mostly because she has been so misbehaved that she has spent most of her time in her room. That has proven to be ineffective with her so we will come up with a new game plan. But never fear that I will shirk my responsibility to her. Now be a good girl, mate and go get our things ready to go home."

He walked away and Darby turned to Megan. "This is not good. Summer hasn't a clue."

"That bad?" asked Megan.

"Yes, remember when Nick spanked you?" Megan nodded. "It's worse. I can't even begin to explain how much worse and that's even if he only uses his hand."

•••••••

Jean-Michel dismissed the guard at the door, asking him to get the others and be prepared to leave when he was done punishing Summer. He opened the door to enter and heard something heavy being thrown at the door. He closed the door and heard it crash. He reopened it and stepped in. This time when she threw something at his head, he caught it.

"Even my Darby knew better than to throw things at her alpha. I can see, little one, that we will need to start from scratch to teach you how to behave as a member of our pack. As we have not been formally introduced, allow me to do so. I am Jean-Michel Gautier, alpha of the New Orleans pack. And you are the newest member of what was the Bae Diogel pack entrusted to my care."

"I don't need or want your instruction."

Jean-Michel chuckled. "I believe that you do not want my instruction or correction. However, it is obvious that you are in need of both. I will give you a choice. You can come to me and formally offer me your fealty as a member of my pack and agree to behave from this time forward. Or, I will put you over my knee, bare your bottom, and give you a spanking that will leave you regretting that decision for days. What is it to be?"

"Fuck you," Summer spat at him.

She looked for something else to throw at him. Taking her eyes off of him would be the first of many regrets she would have. Jean-Michel crossed to her, took hold of her arm, sat down on the bed, and drew her across his knee.

"Lesson one," he said pleasantly. "Little girls do not curse at their alpha or any ranking member of the pack." He landed a hard swat across the middle of her bottom.

"You bastard," she screeched.

"Let's try again," he said, landing three more swats across her backside. "You are a little girl and you do not curse at your alpha, beta, or omega."

"That hurts."

"Good. It was supposed to. And if you think that hurts, you are in for a nasty surprise when I'm through warming up your backside and begin to punish you on your bare bottom."

Having trapped her so that she wasn't able to get away from him, Jean-Michel began to lay down a series of swats to her bottom that made her wail within short order. It didn't take long before Summer was in tears and regretting having crossed the man who now stood as her alpha. He continued to spank her as he laid out what was expected of her.

"Two, little girls do not throw things at people in order to try to hurt them. Three, little girls are to be respectful at all times. You are allowed to speak your mind, but you will do so respectfully and not with a belligerent tone or manner. Four, you will mind me, JD, and Geoff, as well as the other male members of our pack when you are told to do or not to do something. Five, when we get home, you will write a note of apology to both Dylan and to Nick for being such a monumental brat while in their care. Do you understand all that I have said to you?"

"Yes," Summer cried. "Please stop."

"Very well, little one. Let's see if your behavior or attitude have improved." He stopped spanking her and let her rise up from off of his knee. He stood and tilted her chin up to look at him. "You go over to the corner, take your pants off, and stand there and wait for me to give you the rest of your punishment."

"No, please. You said you were through."

"No, I was very clear that what you just received was the warmup to your punishment spanking. I assure you that your new pack and its ranking members take your care and concern and hold them in high regard. You need never worry that your need for structure and correction will not be seen to. Now, take your pants off and go stand in the corner." He turned her toward the corner and gave her a light swat to start her in the right direction. "Go on. Show me you can be a good girl."

Summer walked over to the corner. It had been many years since she'd been disciplined. She'd left her father's pack to escape a forced pairing she didn't want and had been out in the world alone until she had found the pack at Bae Diogel. Once in the corner, she stood facing it.

"Take your pants off, Summer. You don't want me to have to do that for you."

"But…"

He chuckled. "Yes, your butt is going to be a lot more sore when I'm through with it."

She bent down and took off her pants, stomping her foot when she was done.

"Good girls do not stomp their feet. Good girls get their punishment spanking from their alpha just with his hand. Bad girls get a much worse punishment spanking and end up with welts across their bottoms. Do you want to be a good girl?" he asked in a conversational tone. Jean-Michel watched as she struggled. He was glad she could not see the smile he had. The women of the former Bae Diogel pack were strong and proud. He felt lucky to be able to include three of them in his pack. They would add strength and spirit to their line.

"Yes, Alpha," she finally said.

"Very well then." He sat back down on the edge of the bed. "Then come back over to me and I'll finish your spanking. When I'm done, you will pack your things and we will go home."

She turned to look at him. "Please, no?"

He smiled sympathetically and patted his thigh. "Had you greeted me with this attitude, little girl, your spanking would have ended when you were sent to the corner. But I will not allow you to continue to act and lash out at others. So, let's get this done."

"I don't want to."

"Of course you don't. I suspect your bottom is already

on fire and you anticipate, correctly so, that the sting you feel now will only be increased by my spanking your bare bottom. But you need to be spanked well enough that you will think twice before choosing to be naughty again. If you submit to my authority right now, I will only use my hand. Resist your punishment and you will feel my belt across your backside. My Darby would tell you that is not something you wish to have happen. Now, come here and let's get this over with." Again, he patted his thigh.

She stood feeling rooted to the spot. He was right in that her butt was on fire and she could feel both the heat and the swelling starting. She didn't want to submit to a more thorough punishment, but also did not doubt for a minute that he would take his belt to her. He reached out his hand toward her, beckoning with his fingers.

"Please, Alpha. I don't need to be spanked any more. You spank harder than Nick. I'll behave."

He smiled and felt genuine regret that he would have to finish what he had started. "I'm glad to hear that, Summer. But you do need to be spanked further and I will see to it. I'm going to count to three and if you are not standing between my legs waiting for me to pull your panties down to bare your bottom for my discipline, then I will assume you wish to continue being a bad little girl and will take my belt off to use on you."

Again, he held out his hands and beckoned her to come to him. She started to cry.

"One," he said slowly. "Two."

Reluctantly she put one foot in front of the other until she was standing between his legs. He turned her so that she was situated to be put back across his knee. He reached up and tugged her panties down to her knees, before helping her back into position.

"Good girl," he said softly as he began to spank her already pinked globes. She tried to reach back to protect them, but he caught her hands in his one of his and pinned them to the middle of her back. "That's naughty, Summer.

When you get a spanking, you do not reach back to protect your backside."

"It hurts," she cried.

"I know. And it will be even more painful before I'm finished with you. But let this be a lesson that you do not want to continue to go down the road you have traveled since you got here." He increased the strength of the blows being delivered to her bottom, which quickly turned a deep shade of red. She had gone limp over his knee and was sobbing that she could and would behave better. Sensing he had gotten through to her, Jean-Michel stopped and then rubbed her backside soothingly. "I think you've learned your lesson, haven't you, Summer?"

"Yes, Alpha. Please be done."

"I will let this be the end of the actual spanking. I'm going to let you up. You go back to the corner and stand there with your panties around your knees. Can you do that?"

"Yes, Alpha."

He let her up and she obediently went to the corner and stood. He sat for a minute. She made no move to pull up her panties or to soothe her own bottom. At some point she'd been taught to mind. He wondered what had brought her to this point. But he felt heartened to know it didn't appear that it would take much more to make her well behaved.

"Summer?"

"Yes, Alpha?"

"I'm going to leave you now. I want you to put back on some form of pants. My Darby prefers to go without panties right after a spanking and to wear something loose and soft against her derriere. But that is up to you. Please pack your things and be ready to leave within the half hour. Can you do that for me?"

"Yes, Alpha."

He chuckled and walked over to her in the corner. He turned her around and kissed her forehead. "Do not give me a reason to spank you again, little one. Now be a good girl and let's go home."

He left her and went to see to his own mate.

•••••••

Jean-Michel walked up to the main residence and jogged up the stairs. He opened the door, not knowing what to expect. As he had feared, Darby had worked herself into a state.

"Is she all right? You didn't hurt her too badly, did you? How could you do that? I told you she was upset and scared. Couldn't you have let me deal with it?"

He wrapped her in his arms and held her close until she ceased struggling against him. "I know, beloved. You didn't want to see your friend punished. When we get home tonight, you can go upstairs and speak with her. I suggest that you remind her that she is no longer Bae Diogel, but rather pack of New Orleans and subject to my authority."

"Shit, Jean-Michel."

He swatted her backside. "Careful, mate. While I love that you are concerned about Summer, I will not let you slide back into bad behavior."

She glared at him and then her eyes softened as did her smile. "I'm sorry. I know you were doing what you thought was best."

"And?" he said, knowing that wasn't all of it.

"I would prefer not to say."

"And I would prefer that you did."

"But I would prefer not to get in trouble."

"Why? What have you done?" She reached up to pull his mouth down for a kiss. He chuckled. "Nice try, mate. But you tell me now or Summer will not be the only one to need an extra pillow for the trip home."

"I haven't done anything. I was just feeling something I realize I shouldn't."

He chuckled again. "What's the matter, mate, were you

worried I would return aroused from having spanked Summer because spanking you always leaves me in that painful state? Tell me the truth."

"Yes, but I realize that wasn't worthy of you. And I am sorry to ever have thought it."

He kissed her again. "Naughty mate. I shall have to correct your erroneous thinking when we get home. I shall have to prove to you that the only one for whom I grow hard and/or form a knot is the one I hold in my arms."

She smiled seductively and wrapped her arms around his neck. "And how, pray tell, will you do that, my beloved?"

"I shall have to mount you and ride you hard repeatedly."

"And will you finally force your knot into me?"

"Would you like me to knot and tie you?"

She nodded her head.

"Are you sure?"

"Very much so. I understand that when one is with her fated mate it is an exquisite sensation beyond compare."

He held her close and whispered, "I promise, beloved, the brief pain you will have to endure as I force the knot will be forgotten in the aftermath of being knotted and tied to your fated mate."

CHAPTER ELEVEN

The members of the New Orleans pack gathered on the driveway and bid adieu to their hostess. Dylan felt that it might be best if they took their leave early as he anticipated some push back for the New Orleans pack leaving with three of the eight women from Bae Diogel.

Summer was very subdued, but seemed calm. Both Meg and Darby were close by her side and seemed to be taking good care of her.

Jean-Michel kissed both of Skylar's cheeks in farewell. "She will be safe with us."

Skylar looked at him and smiled. "Yes, but when will she be comfortable?"

He returned her smile. "As soon as she learns to behave. And I think we made great headway in that area this morning. Do not worry about your girls, Skylar. They are my pack now and I care for those who are my family."

"I know you do, Jean-Michel. Thank you for all you have done and will do for them. I've never seen Megan or Darby happier. I think even Summer is going to start coming around. We are here if you have need of us."

"And like the young wolf out of Savannah," said Jean-Michel, "should Calon Gwyllt have need, please know that the pack of New Orleans stands with you. You and yours are always welcome in the Crescent City. I am deeply in your and Dylan's debt for allowing my pack to have the honor of adding such beauty, grace, strength, and spirit to my line."

Turning to Darby, Skylar said with a huge smile, "You are so screwed. You are never, ever going to be able to stay mad at him or get the upper hand. He is too charming for words."

"Now you tell me," Darby said, giggling. "And you've only been up against his verbal skills. Trust me, that's nothing compared to his physical and sexual ones."

Jean-Michel swatted her, causing her to squeak in surprise, and shook his finger at her in mock indignation.

Skylar hugged her friend tightly and then embraced her mate as well.

•••••••

The plane was ready and waiting when the members of the New Orleans pack got to the airport. They were ushered out onto the tarmac and were in the air within a very short span of time.

"Oh, I could get used to no waiting, no TSA, and comfy seats," sighed Darby.

"Comfy for some of you," muttered Summer.

Jean-Michel growled at her. "Enough, Summer. If you don't think you can behave for the trip home without some further instruction on how you will behave as a member of this pack, I will have JD take you to the back of the plane. We'll see if he can explain things in a way that you can more easily understand. Is that what you want?"

"You wouldn't dare," she seethed.

The other three men of the New Orleans pack shook their heads and laughed quietly. While Jean-Michel was often indulgent to the women of the pack, he would not tolerate the behavior Summer had exhibited thus far. "You will find, little girl, there is very little I wouldn't dare to keep my pack safe and happy. Now, would you like to behave or should JD take you to the back and give you another spanking?"

"No, Alpha. I'll behave."

"Good, then you can start by apologizing to my mate."

"That's not necessary, Jean-Michel," said Darby, trying to figure out how to help defuse the situation. JD put his hand on her knee and when she looked at him, he shook his head, warning her to stay out of it.

"If she doesn't feel…" started Summer.

"My mate is kind-hearted and inclined to be indulgent with bad behavior—mostly because she is so fond of exhibiting it herself." He leaned over and kissed Darby. "But, she is mate to your alpha and you will show her the respect she is due." Despite JD's warning, Darby started to protest. "Darby," Jean-Michel growled, "do I need to take *you* to the back of the plane?"

"Not unless there is a bed back there you'd like to make use of."

There was a shocked silence and then everyone, including Summer, burst out laughing.

Jean-Michel looked at her and grinned. He waved his finger at her. "You, my beloved, are a most naughty mate."

"Yes, Jean-Michel," she said quietly, all the while grinning at him like a Cheshire cat.

The rest of the trip home was uneventful. The newest pack members were surprised to see that the estate boasted not only a private runway for the jet, but a helicopter pad. Both Darby and Megan sat looking out the windows of the plane. Their respective mates pointed out various landmarks in the New Orleans area as well as different things on the estate itself.

"Shit, Jean-Michel, you weren't kidding when you said we were filthy rich," exclaimed Darby.

"So, you forgive me for only have a jet plane that holds ten?" he teased.

She giggled and turned to look at him. "Yes, but only

because you're great in the sack."

He laughed and leaned forward to nuzzle her neck. "You wait until I get you in our bed, mate."

"Can we skip dinner and go straight to dessert?"

"Do not tempt me, mate. The rest of our pack is anxious to meet all of you. You most especially."

She turned again to him. "Why me?"

"Because we have been waiting years for our alpha to find his mate. Who knew you were up on a deserted island off the coast of North Carolina?" teased JD. "We began to worry that he would never find you, and he refused to settle for anything less than a fated mate."

"Had I known where you were, beloved, I would have had you in my bed years ago."

He saw a dark shadow pass behind her eyes. "Years ago I would not have been in North Carolina. I would have been with the one whose mark you tore from my body." She touched the healing scar lightly.

Jean-Michel leaned across and kissed the scar before kissing her. "Then I would have had the pleasure of killing him in order to claim you as mine. Are you sure you don't want his head on a platter?"

The shadows lifted from her eyes. "Yes, my beloved. I would not have you sully your name or reputation for something that no longer matters and the memory of which fades every time you touch me."

•••••••

The plane came to a stop in front of what Darby assumed was the rest of the New Orleans pack. Jean-Michel led the group off of the plane and introduced the three newest members of the pack to the others. Darby was quite certain she would never learn all of their names. The pack consisted of four, now six, mated pairs, several children, and seven unmated males, two of which had been at the Calon Gwyllt house party. Darby was drawn into the group of well-wishers and looked back to see that Megan was holding Summer's hand and trying to reassure her. Summer looked like cornered prey, and JD was keeping a sharp eye on her.

Darby watched as a shaggy-haired blond, about Jean-Michel's height but with not quite as much musculature, separated from the group and greeted JD and then Megan.

"Jean-Michel?" He turned and gave her his full attention. "Is that Geoff?" He nodded. "Hmmm, you may not get to make a decision about that," she said, pointing to how he took Summer's hand in his.

Jean-Michel smiled. "I told you I had a feeling about that," he whispered. Turning back to the people who surrounded them, he said, "I know you would not welcome us back home without a feast planned for this evening. Let's show these nice southern belles from North Carolina how to celebrate. *Laissez les bons temps rouler!*"

"What?" asked Darby.

"Let the good times roll. It's a way of life in New Orleans. I think for all your freedom, *ma choue*, the women at Bae Diogel did not always lead a celebratory life. Here, we celebrate whenever we can. That way when the difficult times come, as they always do, we have the memories to sustain us and remind us that we have more to which we can look forward."

JD, Megan, Geoff, and Summer joined the group as they headed toward the main house. It was a large white mansion with an expansive patio and a fountain. Summer tried to hang back, but Geoff urged her forward. The grounds were exquisite and the house sat on the banks of the mighty Mississippi River. Like Calon Gwyllt, Darby could see a boathouse and several docks. There was a sailboat, two powerboats, and two airboats.

"Will you take me for a ride on one of the airboats?" she asked.

"But of course. Do you enjoy the water?"

"Very much. I didn't grow up on it, but I learned to love it when I was with Bae Diogel."

They strolled up to the house and were greeted by the staff of the estate. There was a general manager, a housekeeper and her small staff, and a chef and her staff. There were also assorted groundskeepers and stable hands as the pack maintained a small group of riding and carriage horses. Most of the positions had been in the same families for generations. Those who worked for the Gautiers tended to be loyal and were treated so well they never wanted to leave. The family/pack also took care of those who retired in their service in fine form.

The housekeeper, Mrs. Hastings, and the cook, Claudine, requested to speak to the new mistress of the pack at her convenience. Darby was struck by how warm and welcoming everyone was. She was gladdened to see that both Megan and Summer were being engaged by their new pack as well.

Jean-Michel hugged her close. "See? You had nothing to worry about. I knew they would love you."

She looked up at him. "How did you know I was concerned?"

"I told you, the men of our pack are very sensitive to their mates. You will find it difficult to keep a secret from me." He turned to the others, who were getting comfortable in the main room. "We are happy to be home with you. Let's let the newest members of our family have a bit of time to rest and get acclimated to the house. Alex?"

"Jean-Michel?"

"Would you see that Summer's things are put into the guest room here in the main house. Summer, I think you will find it quite pleasant. It has a private bath and balcony. Do I need to leave someone outside your door or do you think you can behave now that you are home?"

"This is not my home," she said.

While Jean-Michel wished she might have spoken differently, he was encouraged that she had spoken in a respectful tone.

"But it is, little one, unless there is no one here with

whom you could be happy. Then we shall try to find you someone who will make you as happy as my Darby has made me. So do I need to leave a guard on your door?"

"You're going to do whatever you want to do."

"Yes," he said quietly. "I am. Geoff, see that someone is posted outside Summer's door at all times. She is not to be allowed to get into mischief. She has a bad habit of thinking she can run amok."

"I'm sure we can convince her there is plenty to like about being here," said Geoff. "Is she confined to her room?"

"No, she can have the run of the estate, provided someone is with her at all times. When she chooses to stay in her room or is ordered to be there, I want someone outside the door or in her room." He turned to Darby. "I need to speak with JD and Geoff briefly. Will you and Megan be all right?"

"We're not fragile little lambs led to the slaughter," she teased.

"Damn," said a very pretty dark-haired woman. "And here I was hoping for a tasty snack."

"Best be careful," said Darby. "You forget that we were part of a pack of females that fought off a rogue European pack and sent the ones we didn't kill home with their tails between their legs." Her hand on his chest stayed Jean-Michel and reminded him that while she was his beloved mate, she was also a capable fighter who knew no fear. "I am mate to your alpha; do not forget yourself with me."

The woman dropped her eyes. The man at her side spoke. "Please forgive Gretchen. She has acted as mistress of the pack before Jean-Michel found you. It seems she has forgotten her place." He turned to his mate. "Gretchen, you apologize right now."

She looked up at Darby and smiled when all she saw was kindness in her eyes. "I am sorry, mistress."

"Darby is fine, Gretchen. And it must be a bit disconcerting for you. I've never been the lady to a great pack before. I'm sure I'll fuck it up." Gretchen and several of the other women giggled as Jean-Michel rolled his eyes. "Do me a favor and give me the benefit of your experience?"

Gretchen smiled at her. "I would be pleased to do so. We're actually a very informal pack and I'm sure you'll be wonderful."

Darby turned back to the man at her side. "Alex, wasn't it?" He nodded. "Please don't feel you have to discipline Gretchen. We're going to be great friends, aren't we?"

Gretchen nodded. "Yes, I believe we are."

JD shook his head. "This isn't good, Jean-Michel, the females are already conspiring together."

"Damn straight," said Megan. "And two of us are good with weapons."

"Careful, boys," said a very pregnant strawberry blonde. "If you're not careful, they'll teach us all and we'll rise up against you and the old guard at the Council." There was general laughter amongst the women.

Jean-Michel grinned. It seemed his pack had taken its newest members into the fold. "Control your women, mate," he said, laughing.

"Oh, I think we're doing just dandy, don't you, ladies?"

There was general agreement and more laughter from everyone.

JD shook his head. "I told you that one of yours was trouble."

"With a capital T," agreed Jean-Michel. He watched as Summer edged quietly toward the door. When she turned, it was Geoff standing in her way. He looked over her head to Jean-Michel, who nodded. "Apparently, Summer feels the need to spend some time in her room."

JD shook his head and started toward her.

"Not to worry, JD. I've got her. I'll take first watch outside her door as soon as we talk to Jean-Michel. Alex, can you show Summer to her room and stay up there until I come up?"

"Sure thing, Geoff." Alex crossed the room and took Summer by the upper arm. "Let's go upstairs before you get yourself in real trouble."

Jean-Michel turned to Gretchen. "Would you be kind enough to show both Darby and Megan to the rooms they share with JD and me?"

"It would be my pleasure. Ladies, if you'll come with me."

They ascended the grand staircase that led up from the main foyer.

"Shit, Dar," Megan whispered. "Did you ever?"

Darby giggled. "Not in my wildest dreams."

Gretchen turned back to them. "I know, isn't it just gorgeous? The whole place has been in the Gautier family for hundreds of years. It's really heaven on earth."

Gretchen opened a door to a huge suite with a large bedroom, sitting room, walk-in closet, and master bath. It was impeccably done but, like the rest of the house, not overly formal but beautiful and elegant in a casual old-world way.

"Good lord, Darby. It's a good thing Jean-Michel likes to keep you close. You could lose him in here."

Gretchen laughed. "Oh, this isn't Jean-Michel and Darby's room; this is yours and JD's."

"Holy shit," breathed Megan as she walked in the room and twirled around.

"We'll leave you to get comfortable. If you need anything just holler or dial 1, that'll get you to one of the staff members. Come on, Darby. I think you're going to love the room you'll share with Jean-Michel."

At the end of the corridor was a set of double doors, Gretchen threw them open. The first thing that Darby saw was a commanding view of the Mississippi. The whole back wall was nothing but French doors and transom lights. It was as if the whole thing was made of glass and yet was still in keeping with the centuries-old mansion. The room was huge, almost twice as big as Megan's new room. The double doors from the hall were to the side of the room and a large, ornate iron bed was to the left as you came in. It had been situated in order to take full advantage of the view.

Darby shook her head. "The pack I was in before Bae Diogel… I don't think the front room was as big as this suite. It's kind of mind-boggling."

Gretchen touched her arm. "Geoff shared with us some of y'all's background. I'm so sorry your first mate was such a bastard. Jean-Michel will kill him if you want…"

"So he says."

"No. Seriously, Darby. He'll kill him if you want and may do it anyway. He's very protective of those he loves. That this man hurt you won't sit well with him."

"I believe that. But I don't need him to. He's given me everything I need. I wear his mark proudly where once I had a mark that brought me nothing but sorrow and shame."

"The shame was never yours."

Darby smiled at her. "As I said… I think we're going to be great friends."

Gretchen giggled. "Me too. I'll leave you to get settled. I think they may have already brought your things up here."

Darby laughed. "That wouldn't take long. We burned most everything we had in our attempt to get away. But now I wonder what it was I thought I was running from."

"Well, the shopping in New Orleans is amazing and your mate is a very, very generous man."

"I know. And not just with his money."

Gretchen nodded. "No, not just with his money. As I said to Megan, just holler if you need anything or use the phone and hit 1." She walked to the door. "Darby? We're awfully glad Jean-Michel found you and brought you home."

•••••••

Jean-Michel and JD quickly brought Geoff up to speed on the house party at Calon Gwyllt and their concerns about trouble coming that might involve their pack as well.

Jean-Michel assured his two lieutenants that they would handle whatever came their way. "I do want security stepped up. Dylan was concerned, rightfully so I believe, that some may come and try to wrest Summer from her new home. That I will not allow. Geoff, see what our friends in some of the smaller packs can find out and if they can give us early warning that trouble is headed our way, tell them I will reward them handsomely."

Geoff laughed. "So, you went up there to bring home a sweet, willing omega and instead ran to ground a female with lots of alpha tendencies and a bad attitude… which I must say you seemed to have brought into good control."

Jean-Michel and JD both laughed. "She has decided she wants to be my mate and may be behaving at the moment, but I will never have complete control over her. And I'm fine with that. She has a beautiful bottom that I will gladly turn a deep shade of red when she is naughty."

Geoff turned to JD. "Correct me if I'm wrong, but weren't you the guy who went with him so one of you could keep your head and we wouldn't piss off the Ruling Council any more than we normally do?"

JD grinned. "That was the plan. What can I say, the heart wants what it wants. I feel very fortunate that both Jean-Michel and Dylan were willing to thumb their noses at the Council and allow me to claim Megan. I owe you for that one, old friend."

"It was my pleasure. I believe our pack will be stronger with the addition of the three of them. What say you, Geoff?"

"I'm sure I don't know what you're talking about."

Both JD and Jean-Michel laughed. "Any trouble here while we were gone?"

"None. We've been a very dull pack. I'm sure with the addition of the three Bae Diogel women that will change. Seriously, do you worry about them causing trouble with the other girls?"

Jean-Michel shook his head. "They may cause some mischief, but no real trouble. I know Darby will be far too tired and sore from her mate's constant and repeated lovemaking."

JD sobered. "Do you plan to claim her completely tonight?"

"I do. I wanted to wait until I'd marked her and had her at home. I will stay close to her for the next few days and may even work and have our meals brought to our room."

"What do you want to do about Summer?" asked JD.

Jean-Michel thought for a moment. "She didn't actually get away… but only because we were vigilant. JD, speak with her and see what you think. I'm fine with whatever you decide to do."

"I'm inclined to give her a spanking she won't forget any time soon. I know you spanked her last night, but I also know that you didn't use a strap or a belt. No one at Calon Gwyllt did either. I think she needs a good welting to get through her thick head that her old life is over and she needs to settle down. The last thing we need is her running away and causing trouble. Dylan doesn't need that and neither do we."

"You're being awfully quiet, Geoff. Nothing to contribute?"

"Discipline of the unmated girls is JD's area of responsibility."

"It is the responsibility of whoever I deem it to be. What I'm asking you is how you feel about him spanking her?"

Geoff grinned at both of them. "I wasn't that obvious, was I? I'd hate the other men in our pack to think that the ranking members pulled one of the old guard's tricks of keeping the best for themselves."

"Regardless of what anyone thinks, that isn't what happened. The question is how do you feel about my giving her a good hard welting? Taking that cute little bottom and turning it bright red before laying welts across it?"

Geoff couldn't suppress the low growl coming from his

throat.

JD laughed. "Yeah, that's what I thought."

"I suppose that answers that. I'd like a chance to talk to the rest of the pack. I really don't want to cause bad feelings. There may be others who feel called to her."

Jean-Michel laughed. "Of course you do. That is why you are our most excellent omega—the peacekeeper. I will leave it to the two of you to decide on Summer's punishment and which of you will administer it. But, she needs to be taken to task for her last little stunt. I do not want the pack to feel as though we're on constant lockdown because of her foolishness."

CHAPTER TWELVE

Darby was standing on the balcony taking in the view of both the Mississippi and the estate she would now call home. She shook her head. She was amazed at how much things could change in such a short time. She remembered the desperation they had felt when the edict from the Ruling Council had reached them. They had tried to get away, but to what?

She felt his presence even before he opened the door. She turned around to face him, leaning against the ornate balcony railing.

"Planning another escape, beloved?"

She smiled. "The only running I plan to do is straight into your arms whenever you leave me for too long," she said as she launched herself across the room.

He caught her up and kissed her hungrily. "I missed you too. Are you happy to be home?"

"How could I not be? I have a gorgeous man who keeps me happy and sated. And I've been accepted into a well-respected and thriving pack. I was just wondering what it was I thought I was running from?"

He kissed her gently. "I think more from the unhappiness of your past than toward anything in your future." He saw doubt creep into her eyes. "What?"

"Nothing," she said, smiling brightly.

He swatted her backside twice with considerable heat. "What did I tell you about lying to me?"

She shook her head and kissed him. "I'm sorry. I just don't want to add to the load I know you carry as alpha with my silly concerns."

"Your concerns are never silly to me. Do you want to amend your answer now or do you need to have a well-soaped mouth and bright red backside before you share them with me?"

She giggled. "I think I'll choose to amend my answer. I want to be a good mate to the alpha of our pack. I was only kind of kidding when I told Gretchen I'd probably fuck it up."

"Gretchen fucked it up plenty of times," he said, chuckling. "Do not worry. One of the tenets of our pack is that unless someone dies, we can fix it. Do your best; ask for help. Never fear that anyone here will judge you. And anyone who is not of our pack does not have an opinion that matters."

"I do want to please you. God, I can't believe I just said that, not to mention that I meant it."

"You do please me, *ma choue*. I am happier than I have ever been. There is no one who has seen us together who would dispute that. You complete me. I have been waiting for you my whole adult life."

Tears welled in her eyes.

"I do not tell you this to upset you."

"I know," she said quietly. "I just don't feel as though I'm worthy. You needed a Skylar—a woman who has been mistress to a great pack. One who is gracious and smart and kind. I'm only smart… and even that one is iffy at times."

He swatted her again. "You couldn't be more wrong. There wasn't anyone downstairs who didn't see how gracious and kind you were to Gretchen. You would have been well within your rights to ask to have her punished for the way she spoke to you. Instead you made her laugh, defused any tension that might have been forming, and offered to be her friend. If any of them had their doubts about my rogue-wolf bride, you allayed their concerns."

"What about yours?"

He laughed. "My only concerns about you have always been how to keep you safe and prevent you from running away. I do not think I need worry about the latter anymore."

She shook her head. "No, beloved. I'm afraid you're stuck *with* me. And as soon as you get us both naked and that knot I can feel deep inside me, you'll be stuck *to* me."

"You are a most naughty mate."

She giggled.

"There will be some kind of celebratory dinner this evening. If you wish to attend, I will wait to bury my knot in you. If not, I will attend to your desire to be mine completely."

"Will they think badly of me if I prefer to spend my first evening in bed with my mate?"

"No, they will think your mate the luckiest of men. Is that what you prefer?" She nodded. He released her and walked to the phone, calling the general manager of the plantation. "Vachon? Your mistress and I will not be joining everyone this evening. Please let Geoff know. I'm not sure if JD will be in attendance either. Have Claudine send someone up with our meals until further notice. Thank you."

"Oh, God, they're all going to know why we didn't come down tonight," she said, only slightly exaggerating her embarrassment.

He chuckled as he pulled her back into his arms. "They would have known anyway when they saw how happy their alpha was. Nothing quite keeps an alpha happy and focused as being able to knot and tie his true mate on a regular basis."

"But, until further notice?"

He tucked a long strand of her blonde hair behind her

ear. "Yes, *ma choue*. I mean to claim you repeatedly."

She looked at him and saw the smile in his eyes and the grin on his face. "I see. You're so sure I'm going to like this whole knotting and tying thing?"

"I am," he said with confidence. "I will ensure that you desire it above all things." He nuzzled her neck and whispered in her ear, "As do I."

"Then what are you waiting for?" she asked as she kissed him, slipping her tongue into his mouth and coaxing his tongue to come and dance with hers.

He led her to their bed and drew back the covers. "Do you want help getting naked for me?"

She giggled. "I'm beginning to think you like the fact that I have so few clothes so I'm either in one of your shirts or naked."

He smiled. "It does have its advantages." He began to undress her. She closed her eyes and shuddered in response. "Relax, *ma choue*, there is nothing to fear."

"He hurt me every time he did it to me. I never found any joy or pleasure from it."

"I know, beloved, but I promise you that you will find great amounts of both from our joining. The pain will be brief but the pleasure intense and long. Would you prefer to wait a bit longer? I have no desire to pressure you."

She shook her head. "No, I want to be yours completely. Not only do I understand that it is painful for you to continually suppress your knot, but that it isn't good for you to do so. I want desperately to give you that, but still…"

"I know, beloved. But I am, in this regard, a patient man. I want you to be as desirous of our ultimate joining as I am and will wait until you are."

"But I am. I don't just want it for you. I want it for me too. So please, Jean-Michel, claim me completely."

He kissed her gently, but with a wealth of passion behind it. "I will, my beloved, and you will forget that you ever feared it." He finished undressing her and then quickly removed his own clothes before sliding between the sheets next to her.

Jean-Michel pulled her to him. He was happy to see that her concerns weren't too deeply seated as she was as soft and compliant as he had come to expect. Her body molded perfectly to his and she responded to his touch with a fiery passion of her own.

He cupped her breast in his hand and squeezed it gently. She moaned in appreciation. He lowered his head to take her nipple in his mouth. She cradled his head in her hands and pushed her tit deeper into his mouth.

Jean-Michel ran his hand down between her legs. He stopped for a moment to rub her clit, causing her to buck her hips in response. He released the nipple on which he had been suckling and transferred his attention to the other. His hand moved down to test her level of arousal. His mate was very, very wet and her labia felt swollen. He pressed two fingers into her wet channel and felt her pussy clamp down on them as she came.

"Jean-Michel," she called quietly.

"Yes, my beloved?" he said, gazing into her face while he began pumping her pussy. He could feel her body quickly ramping back up to another climax. "It would appear, my sweet, that you have been too long without your mate's cock doing the job of my fingers."

"Yes," she moaned. "Please?"

"I think you are not quite ready for me."

"Yes, I am," she demanded.

He removed his fingers from her core and swatted between her legs with more than a bit of sting.

"Shit. That hurts."

"Yes, but deserved when a naughty mate forgets her place and tried to demand instead of ask. Would you prefer I go back to fingering you, or does your pussy prefer to get the same treatment you bottom does when you misbehave?"

She sighed. "Please don't spank me there. I'll behave, it's just I want you. I need to feel you fill me up, to stroke me so that all that exists is you and me. Please don't keep me waiting and don't make me beg."

He nuzzled her and smiled at her once more, taking her nipple deep into his mouth. He sucked hard and she cradled his head. His hand stole down her body and began to play again with her clit, causing her to undulate her hips in response. As her breathing quickened, he moved from swirling his fingers around her clit to pressing his thumb against it and slipping his fingers back within her pussy.

This time her response was to spread her legs wider and her pelvis tilted upward as if to present her pussy to him for his use.

"There's my good mate," he crooned. "Look at me, Darby."

She opened her eyes and held his gaze.

"Who am I?"

"My fated mate," she said with a sigh. "The guy who takes fiendish delight in denying me what we both want desperately."

He chuckled. She giggled and nuzzled him.

He moved down her body stopping to kiss, lick, and suck as he went. He spent considerable time pleasuring both of her nipples until they were so hard they bordered on painful. He kissed, licked, and sucked his way down her body. Finally, he had his head between her legs. He nuzzled her clit, causing her to begin to once again move her hips. He swirled his tongue around her and then sucked her swollen nub into his mouth where he nipped and suckled it. Darby's hips began to move with more strength and speed. Jean-Michel responded by using his tongue as he had his fingers and plunged it in and out of her. She bucked wildly against his onslaught. He felt her pussy clamp down on his tongue and she called his name as she came for him again.

Jean-Michel raised up and began to kiss his way back up her body. As he did so, he slipped two fingers back into her channel and began to slowly move them back and forth as his thumb pressed against her clit. Her body once again began to ascend to its peak and he settled himself between her legs. He brought both of his hands up to take a firm hold of her hips. He felt her stiffen in anticipation of the pain.

"It will be all right, Darby," he said in a soothingly seductive voice. "Try to relax, sweetheart."

He knew that any further delay would only give her more time to be become anxious. His mouth descended onto hers, capturing it as he surged forward, growling low and deep within his throat. He only vaguely felt her body try to deny his entrance. The strength of his thrust ensured that his knot was forced up inside her.

He could feel her pussy tighten as the knot stretched her and heard her sharply inhaled breath. He knew that for them to experience the intimacy and sensuality of the knot and resulting tie, she would experience pain at his hands.

He held her tight and stilled within her. He could feel her channel clamp down on him in response to his invasion as he kissed her and murmured words of love and encouragement to her. Slowly, she began to relax and he felt her pussy accommodate his knot. She quit struggling but seemed unsure of what would come next.

"That's the worst of it, sweetheart. It will be all right, love. I promise the pleasure that is about to begin will obliterate all thoughts of your discomfort."

Slowly, but surely, he felt the pull of her sheath drawing him forward and down into the floor of her pussy. He watched her face as recognition set in that he was no longer causing her pain. That recognition led to wonder as the knot began to swell and lock her body to his.

"Oh, my God," she sighed in pleasure. She looked into his eyes and he could see the love and desire he had for her reflected back to him. She wound her arms around his neck and raised the upper portion of her body to his to kiss him and rub her hardened nipples against his chest.

He chuckled, enjoying her wanton response to his possession. The thought that he would have no trouble convincing his mate to be knotted on a frequent basis flashed through his mind. He gathered her close and then stretched her back down in their bed. He began to move his hips in the rhythm of love. Sealed to her as he was, the movement was more of a rocking nature than a true stroking.

He watched her eyes roll back in her head as she gave herself over to his passion. She climaxed repeatedly as she dug her nails into his back. She called his name as her pussy spasmed around his cock and its knot repeatedly. He could feel his cum rolling up from his balls and through the knot as it targeted the back wall of her core and began spurting out in great ropes. Her body arched and molded to him and she cried out for him, lost in her own desire. His cock continued to pump his seed deep into her body. Finally, he had emptied himself in her and was still.

He settled himself on top of her and kissed her gently. "Are you all right, *ma choue*?"

She gazed up at him lovingly. "All right doesn't even begin to cover it. That was amazing and this? This is, I don't even know how to describe what this is, but I like it too."

He smiled, enjoying her response. "This is the most sensual and intimate act you will ever experience. And given your response, I think my mate will experience it on a very regular basis."

She smiled and nodded as she kissed him passionately and wound her legs with his… in essence locking her to him as surely as his engorged and sealed knot bound her to him. They began to share the stories of their childhoods, which were in sharp contrast to one another.

Jean-Michel had experienced an idyllic childhood here on the plantation. He had been raised, alongside JD, Geoff, and several others, in the pack to which he now stood as alpha. His father had been alpha before him and happily mated to his mother until she had passed.

Jean-Michel said with a wistful sigh, "He didn't want to live without her. He willed himself to die and was gone within six months."

"I'm so sorry, my love."

"Don't be. I was sorry that they were gone, but happy that they were together."

Darby's upbringing had been in a small farming community with a small pack that could barely keep its head above water. They might have done better if her weak-willed father hadn't been a compulsive gambler who got into heavy debt. That debt had been to another hard-scrabble pack's alpha who wanted her father's pretty blonde daughter to breed future generations of his line. The fact that he was never able to get her pregnant was a constant source of irritation to him. He had knotted her whenever a knot began to form but not in a way that would have ensured she would conceive. Several times Jean-Michel growled in response to her ill treatment.

She found that sharing her story with him allowed her to release the anger and pain that had always accompanied it. His loving response to her pain allowed her to put it in the past and focus instead on soothing his ire and opening her heart even more to him.

Jean-Michel laughed when she began to quiz him about how often a knot would form and how often he would share it with her.

"As often as you will have me. I have no desire to share it with anyone else. And you no longer worry that when I want to bury myself deep within you it will hurt?"

She giggled. "Don't get me wrong, your forcing that thing in me is incredibly painful. But Skylar was right, what's waiting on the other side of that brief flash of pain more than makes up for it. So, no, mate, I no longer fear anything about you or your mighty knot."

Jean-Michel told her stories of their pack's history and accomplishments. Some were inspiring, some humorous, and some showed the great strength the pack had always had to stand as one and survive. Finally, the knot began to dissipate and he eased himself from her.

She had been dozing and made a feeble protest.

"Shh, *ma choue*. Sleep. I will be close by."

He could hear her breathing deepen as sleep overtook her. He glanced at the clock and realized he had been tied to her for a bit more than three hours. It wasn't dark yet, but the sun was beginning to set. He held her close as she slept and allowed her body to rest and recuperate. He knew she would be sore from taking his knot and being tied to him for the first time.

A few hours later, he heard a discreet knock on their door. He eased himself from their bed. Opening the door, he smiled as he found the tray laden with food. He brought it in and set it down on the end of the bed.

As he lifted the cloches from over the dishes he could see Darby's heightened sense of smell kicked in and led her back to wakefulness. Drowsily she sat up and reached first for him, kissing him lazily but deeply.

"What is all of this?"

He chuckled. "This is Claudine's idea of a light repast. You will find our chef never wants anyone to be hungry. Specifically, this is shrimp etouffee, jambalaya, gumbo, and her special crab cakes. There are also various side dishes and her peach cobbler as well as hummingbird cake."

"She doesn't expect us to eat all of this tonight, does she?"

"No. This is a bit much even for Claudine. I suspect as she doesn't know your tastes she wanted to ensure there was enough to feed you to allow you to recover from the ordeal of being mated to me."

"If she thinks it's an ordeal," she said, sitting up, wincing, and then crawling across the bed to the food, "she's obviously never fucked you."

"Darby, watch your language. Do not think just because you provide me with the ultimate pleasure in this life, that I will not spank that pretty bottom when it's needed."

She stuck her fingers into the peach cobbler, taking a bite for herself and offering him the rest, which he willingly sucked off her fingers. "And I suppose you're the one who decides when it's needed?"

"The one and only."

CHAPTER THIRTEEN

Jean-Michel and Darby spent the next few days as if they were on their own private honeymoon. Darby giggled that the only piece of clothing he allowed her to wear was one of his shirts and then only when she insisted on going out on the balcony where she might be seen. Other than that Jean-Michel preferred his mate naked and more readily available to his carnal desires. He knotted and tied her numerous times… several times at her instigation. In between the rapture they experienced when so doing, he would mount her with the knot and take long, hard strokes to bring her to repeated orgasms. At one time she casually remarked that her pussy no longer felt normal when his cock wasn't lodged within it.

Darby began leaving Claudine notes of the things brought up to them that she particularly enjoyed. She and Jean-Michel ate at least one of their meals each day on the expansive balcony off their bedroom. It was private and sheltered but had a one-hundred-eighty-degree view of the river. Darby was fascinated that the Mississippi was still used as one of the major causeways to get from New Orleans to other points along the way.

One afternoon when Jean-Michel retrieved their midday

tray, there was a note from JD asking to speak briefly with Jean-Michel at his earliest convenience.

"I fear, *ma choue*, that reality has finally reared its ugly head and there are matters other than you that need my attention."

She smiled and wrapped herself in his arms. "That's all right, beloved. I knew at some point they'd want me to share. Is it all right with you if I leave our room?"

"But of course. I never intended to keep you locked away… forever," he said, smiling. "You do know how much joy you bring to me, don't you?"

"I believe you've mentioned it a time or two… even before I was ready to hear it."

"This is your home. You are free to do whatever you wish."

"Hmmmm… Gretchen mentioned there was great shopping to be had in New Orleans and that my mate was a generous man. As you might recall, I have very few clothes."

He laughed. "Then if it pleases you, go buy a new wardrobe. Take Megan; she probably needs some things too. In fact, why don't you plan an outing with all of the women of our pack for some shopping and whatever else you'd like to do. You haven't gotten to know them, but the women in our pack are a hard-working, fairly frugal lot. Perhaps they will allow you to indulge them more often than they allow their mates or me to do so."

"All of the women… including Summer?"

"If you think Summer can be trusted. I will get Geoff's and JD's opinions on the matter as well. I would prefer she not be segregated and learn to live as a member of this pack."

"Do you think she'll always be with us?"

"I do. Geoff all but admitted he felt called to her the day we arrived home. If he hasn't already done so, this meeting may well be about Geoff wishing to claim her."

"Let me know if I can include her. I agree that as soon

as she can get used to a new normal, the better."

He kissed her briefly as he finished dressing. "I will leave it in your hands, mate. We do have a car and driver so make use of him if you choose."

"We have a limo?" she asked, giggling.

"Yes, but just a small one." He laughed and left her.

Jean-Michel trotted down the steps and was waylaid by the housekeeper, Mrs. Hastings.

"Alpha, is the mistress going to be available today? I have a few things to discuss with her but didn't want to intrude."

"She should be down shortly. Do you know where JD and Geoff might be?"

"They were in having lunch. Thank you, sir. She does know we're so very glad to have her, doesn't she?"

"Yes, Mrs. Hastings. That she does. Everyone has made my mate feel very welcome and I am grateful for that."

Jean-Michel entered the dining hall and was greeted by the majority of the pack. He scanned the room and as he got close to Geoff, he said, "No Summer?"

Geoff shook his head. "No, she's pretty much been in her room since you locked yourself away with your mate. JD and I want to talk to you about her."

"I am at your disposal and would apologize for not attending to the situation sooner, but I fear I am rather enamored of my mate."

"Really? I hadn't noticed."

Both men laughed. Having grown up with his beta and his omega was a decided advantage for Jean-Michel. There was an ease in the relationship between the three of them that rarely existed in ranking pack members.

Jean-Michel looked to JD, who sat with Megan close to his side. He smiled. Megan looked very happy and relaxed in her new home. He crossed over to her.

"Still happy about being mated to this beast?"

She laughed. "Very. Although I've been told should I wish to dissolve that pairing there are others here who would take his place."

"It isn't funny, Meg."

She laughed harder. "Yes, it is. They were only trying to get a rise out of you. However, I much prefer the rise I get when I try… and often when I don't try."

JD growled at her and she kissed him before he could finish. Jean-Michel was tickled to see JD soften and return the kiss. Megan was good for his beta.

"Best be careful, Megan. Not only is he the beta of this pack but your mate. He has the authority to decide in either role to put you over his knee should he decide it would do you some good."

She said nothing, but kissed JD again.

"I had a note that said you wished to speak with Geoff and me? Should we talk here? Darby should be down in a moment, or does the matter require more delicacy and is best discussed in the library?"

He felt her enter the room before he turned and smiled at her.

"We have a library?"

"Yes. My grandfather loved books, in particular, first editions. My father collected paintings."

"And what do you collect, my mate?"

"Only a beautiful blonde with whom I shall spend my life."

Darby rolled her eyes. "Is he always like this?"

"Only since he met you," teased JD.

Darby scanned the room. "No Summer?"

"Alas, Summer continues to avoid happiness at all cost. Sweetheart, why don't you stay with Megan and the rest of the pack; I need to speak with JD and Geoff."

"Anything wrong?"

Both JD and Geoff shook their heads. "Nothing a good welting won't fix," said JD.

The three ranking members headed toward the library.

"What the hell was that about?" asked Darby. She reached up to squeeze Gretchen's hand as she joined them.

"With the exception of Summer, are all the women of the pack here?"

"They are," said Gretchen.

Darby lowered her voice. "The pregnant girl… I can't remember her name."

"Lily."

"Let's all of us go join Lily for a moment."

Gretchen gathered the other two female members of the pack while Darby and Megan went to Lily.

"How are you feeling, Lily?"

"Very pregnant and wondering why I was so happy about this all those months ago when I found out. I'm sorry. I shouldn't be complaining."

"Why ever not? If I'm to lead the women of our pack, who the hell else should you complain to?"

Lily giggled. "My feet are killing me."

"I have an idea about how to fix that." Darby waited until all of the women were sitting together. "Here's the deal. I'm in desperate need of a mani/pedi. My mate, because I'm such a great lay, is in an exceptionally good mood and sort of gave me carte blanche and an open credit card for the rest of the afternoon. Megan and I don't have a lot of clothes. So, what do you say we all go into town, get our fingernails and toes done, and do some serious damage to his credit card? Gretchen tells me the shopping in New Orleans is fabulous and seeing how well dressed you all are, I'm thinking you must know the places to get that done."

They all laughed and agreed to be ready to go in a half an hour. Having overheard part of the conversation, Vachon offered to get the car and driver ready for their excursion.

•••••••

As the doors closed behind them in the library, Jean-Michel said, "Let me guess… Summer has continued in her naughty ways."

JD shook his head. "As bad as she was at Calon Gwyllt, she's been worse. We have a man outside her door and one posted beneath her balcony. After two failed escapes, she has now gone on a hunger strike. Claudine is beside herself."

"I won't chastise you for being with your mate. After all, you came downstairs before I did," Jean-Michel chuckled. "But I fail to see the problem."

"This one," JD said, pointing to Geoff, "refuses to claim the brat and deal with her and has made it clear if I take a strap to her, I'm in for one helluva fight."

"Geoff, she can't be allowed to continue to misbehave. Why haven't you taken her in hand?"

"Because we aren't mated. And because the two of you, who are the only ones to discipline the girls in our pack, were upstairs and not inclined to do anything but pleasure yourselves and your mates. Not that I blame you for that. I haven't claimed her yet so have no rights to her as her mate."

"Why on earth not?" asked a perplexed Jean-Michel.

"I didn't have your blessing. You disappeared upstairs before I could obtain it."

"For Christ's sake, Geoff. When have you ever known me to deny a man his fated mate when he's called to her? If that's the only problem, go get the brat. I'll formally name you her mate and then you can deal with her."

Both Jean-Michel and JD would later agree they had never seen Geoff look so relieved or so happy.

"Thank you, Jean-Michel. For what it's worth I spoke with the other guys who don't have mates and they're fine with it."

JD snorted. "Of course they are, only Jean-Michel and you are foolish enough to want known troublemakers as mates."

"As I recall, *mon ami*, your Megan spent a bit of time over Nick's knee when she was with Calon Gwyllt."

"Yes, but I have yet to have to discipline her. My mate is the model of good behavior."

It was Jean-Michel's turn to snort. "Give her time. That's just the whole newly mated glow talking. Geoff, I believe Darby is going to take the rest of the girls for an outing into the city. Let's make this formal and final before they leave. That way you'll have the afternoon to sort things out with your mate before they return."

"Thank you, Jean-Michel. I'll go get her."

"I'll go round up the rest of the troops," offered JD.

Jean-Michel let them go and was going to go find Darby when she entered the room. "Problem?"

"With Summer. But one that is soon to be remedied. She is to be mated with our omega, Geoff."

"What if she doesn't want to?"

"At the risk of having you rise up to protect one of your own, she doesn't have a say in it. Geoff believes he is her fated mate. And like other members of the notorious Bae Diogel pack, she refuses to heed his call."

"I don't like it, Jean-Michel. She has a right to decide her own fate."

"No, my beloved, she does not. For one, she is Bae Diogel and the Council has spoken on the matter. For two, she is much safer mated than not. And although you do not know him well, I believe you know that Geoff would never be part of a coerced pairing if he wasn't absolutely sure. If you want to make a silent protest and not be in the room when I make the announcement, I will allow you to remain here in the library until after it's done. I would prefer that you and Megan be present, but I will respect and understand if you choose not to be."

"He won't hurt her, will he?"

"Do you mean will he be mean to her or abuse her? No. But apparently, she's been even worse than she was at Calon Gwyllt. Her first few days with her mate will most likely be more like yours than like Megan's. JD believes, and he's usually right about these things, that she needs a good welting before she'll settle down. And as it did wonders for you, I'm inclined to agree with him."

"Can I at least try talking to her?"

"No, beloved. We've gone past that."

They could suddenly hear Summer screeching in the upper hallway as she fought with Geoff, resisting his attempts to bring her downstairs peacefully. Jean-Michel quirked his eyebrow at his mate.

"You may be right. And I will stand with you, mate. I don't know that I think you're right, but I don't know that I think you're wrong."

The pack had assembled in the great hall of the mansion. Jean-Michel entered with Darby at his side. He whispered to JD that if it was going to upset Megan that she need not be present. JD indicated she would stay.

"Let go of me, you overgrown shaggy dog," snarled Summer as she tried to extricate herself from Geoff's grasp.

Jean-Michel laughed. "I think, *mon ami*, your mate is going to need to be instructed in the ways of our pack."

Summer rounded on him. "I'll say whatever the hell I want to say… however I want to say it."

The pack had gone very quiet. While Jean-Michel was a very loving alpha who took the care and responsibility for those of his pack very seriously,, he was not one to tolerate open hostility or disrespect.

"Summer, that's enough…" started Darby.

"Jesus, Darby. Help me. Shake off whatever sex-crazed haze he has you in and help me."

Jean-Michel growled and Darby put her hand on her mate's arm. "Is he great in the sack? You better believe it. Does he have me in some kind of thrall to his power? Perhaps when he's knotted inside me and I'm tied to him for hours at a time. But I assure you that no one has or ever will have control over my thoughts or feelings. Bae Diogel was never about being able to be a bitch. It was about taking care of one another and finding our own way. Maybe that's what led us all here. I get that you're not happy about this. I wasn't happy when Jean-Michel ran me to ground and pinned me underneath him. I sure as hell wasn't happy with him the first time he spanked me and I really hated him the first time he used his belt. But you know what? For every time I was a complete and total bitch, I got punished and forgiven. He never disciplined me harder that he was willing to love me."

"Great. You're well laid and don't mind being beaten again. But I want no part of it. I will not be forced into a pairing not of my own choosing."

"The females of our kind have always been forced into pairings. Some by ranking members in their packs and some by being given the opportunity to run and make a fight for it. Do you really think there's anywhere you could go that there isn't someone who'd be willing to track you down and claim you?"

"I'd rather take my chances out there."

"Really? What if the one who catches and claims you is some alpha who truly didn't believe females were good for anything but knotting and fucking to try to breed them for an heir? Want to know what happens when you don't conceive and you get a period? I'll tell you from firsthand knowledge; you get the shit beat out of you. Not spanked or welted, but some guy twice your size takes his fist and pummels you. Then he throws you over the back of something and fucks you without any kind of foreplay. And if there are other male members of the pack around? So be it. They get to watch and cheer him on. And if he's really drunk and can't get it up, but one of his ranked buddies can, they step in and do the job for him."

Summer looked like someone had punched her in the gut. "Darby, I…"

Darby waved her off. "So don't tell me about taking chances. I don't know Geoff hardly at all, but look around you, Summer… do any of these women look abused or haunted or like they are anything other than happy? No, they do not. They are all loved and cared for. Get the fuck over yourself, Summer and count yourself fortunate that my mate has a big enough heart to love you and call you pack and family in spite of how bloody awful you've been. And that even though you have treated him abominably, that Geoff has the strength of heart and character to listen to his heart when it says you are his true mate."

Geoff took Darby's hand and rubbed his forehead and cheek against it in an age-old show of respect and loyalty.

She turned toward Jean-Michel. "I'm sorry, my love. I should have told you. If you don't want to be mated to me…"

He folded her in his arms. "Shhh," he said soothingly as her kissed her gently. "I suspected the entire story was worse than you let on, but figured you'd tell me when you were ready. You are home now. You have me and the rest of our pack. No one will ever hurt you again."

A comforting and supportive cry went up from the group and they gathered around her.

"Never doubt that nothing you ever did before or was done to you could make me waver in my devotion or the depth of my love for you. You are my fated mate… and I am yours now and forever."

Summer made a sound of disgust. "That's all fine and well for you, but it won't happen to me. I can fight for myself."

"Can you?" piped up Megan. "As I recall when the Serbs came, you were being dragged back to their boat by the roots of your hair until Darby killed the two trying to take her and attacked the two that had you. The way I remember it, if it weren't for Darby, you'd most likely have ended up with that bunch of losers with the whole lot of them breeding you repeatedly."

The pack all looked at their beta's mate questioningly. She smiled and nodded. "Trust me, our alpha doesn't ever really want to piss his mate off… especially if there's a sharp knife anywhere around. We buried six of them at sea… Darby killed three of them, Skylar two, and Roz, our beta, took out the last of them. The rest we sent home licking their wounds and, I'm sure, plotting their revenge."

"That was different," stammered Summer. "We weren't prepared for an attack…"

"Enough," said Jean-Michel calmly. "Like it or not, Summer, you are a member of this pack and subject to my authority. Within that authority I have made the decision to honor Geoff's request to claim you. You have a choice to make. Do you want to accept that perhaps others know what is best for you and accept his claim or do you prefer to run?"

"He could take her into the library and give her the welting she needs to force her acceptance," JD offered. "That seems to have worked for Nick and Bianca of Calon Gwyllt."

"Yes, he could. But I worry that it would be distressing for the other women of our pack. Offering a woman a chance to run is a time-honored tradition in wolf society."

"What are the parameters that allow me to win?" asked Summer, knowing that Skylar's original mate had chased her down for two days.

"Tradition says that for as long as he wants to chase, you must run. I do not feel that offers a woman anything more than the illusion of being able to break free of her pack. So, I will set the parameters at twenty-four hours or the boundaries of our home here at the plantation, whichever is first achieved. Do you have the clothing and footwear that you feel you need to be successful?"

She nodded.

"Then we will gather and you can start your run when the rest of our ladies return from a trip into the city. Until then you will be returned to your room. Geoff, I give you leave to try to persuade your mate that this is not the course she wants to pursue, but you may not discipline her for her naughtiness until after you have caught her or she has accepted your claim, whichever comes first."

JD moved forward and took her by the upper arm to take her back upstairs. "I don't suppose, Jean-Michel, you'd be inclined to let me punish her in the way she needs?"

"No. She is Geoff's and he can see to providing her the structure and correction that she seems to need." Jean-Michel turned to Darby. "Beloved, while you are shopping, please ensure that all of our ladies get several things that please them and start rebuilding Summer's wardrobe as she doesn't have many things either."

"Yes, Alpha, your wish is my command."

He laughed. "Yes, but only because it was what you planned to do anyway."

She giggled. "But, of course. Summer, I'd rest and plot my best way out of here. My money's on Geoff." She reached out and squeezed Geoff's arm. "Now, ladies, there's a car waiting for us and our alpha's money to spend." She kissed Jean-Michel and headed out to the car waiting to take them into the city.

CHAPTER FOURTEEN

Vachon had taken the liberty of securing appointments at one of the nail salons in the city to attend to the ladies of the pack. It was within the French Quarter itself and boasted mimosas, wine, soft drinks, and water for those having services done.

As Darby was sitting in the pedicure chair, one foot in the bubbling water and one being worked on, she turned to Gretchen. "Is Vachon always this good at setting things up on the fly?"

Gretchen nodded. "Yes. He's incredible. I swear if you asked him to get you the keys to the city of Atlantis, with just a bit of notice, he'd pull it off. Someone from his family has been the general manager of the plantation since the time of Jean Lafitte. If you want or need anything, just ask Vachon. Also Mrs. Hastings is the most amazing housekeeper, she runs the staff. She's the virtual iron fist in a velvet glove. And well, you've already tasted Claudine's cooking. By the way, she was just tickled with the notes you sent back with the trays."

Megan leaned over to them from her pedicure chair. "I'm not sure we're ever going to get Lily to leave."

"I heard that," said Lily. "And I do think you can just

leave me here and I will have this nice young lady massage my feet and calves for the rest of the day. Oh, my God, this feels amazing."

Darby arranged for Lily to do just that. The nail technician was tickled to be allowed to just take care of one patron for the rest of the day. Lily seemed more comfortable than she had been for a while. The five remaining female members of the pack left to explore the city's most fashionable shops.

It didn't take long for both Darby and Megan to feel as though they had been friends with the women of their packs for their whole lives. They laughed and teased each other and made a serious dent in the credit card Jean-Michel had given Darby. Darby had been surprised when she took the card out to use it to discover that it was in her name. Jean-Michel must have ordered it the day after he claimed her. As her mate had requested, Darby watched as someone would find something, try it on, and then put it back as being unnecessary. She was having great fun then purchasing it for her anyway.

It had been a lovely afternoon and the five mated women of the pack were headed back to pick up Lily before having the driver take them home. The driver, Jackson, stopped the car in front of the nail salon and relocked the doors before any of the women could get out. He opened the divider between the front and back and said to Darby, "This doesn't look right. There doesn't seem to be any activity and yet the sign says open. Please wait in the car until I come and open the door."

Jackson was right; the lights were on as was the 'Open' sign, but you couldn't see anyone moving around in the salon and Lily was not still perched in the pedicure chair in which they'd left her.

He got out and headed toward the door of the salon. A small group of men who had kept out of sight until then jumped him and made a beeline for the car door. Finding it locked, they pounded on the roof of the car.

Inside the car, Megan looked at Darby. "Is it just me…"

"No, they're some of the bastards from my former mate's pack."

Before Darby could say more, one of them had pulled out a knife and was now threatening to cut their driver's throat.

Darby turned to the other women. "Stay here. Lock the door immediately after me and somebody get on the phone with Jean-Michel."

Megan grabbed her. "Where are you going?"

"To see if I can't buy us some time." Darby dislodged Megan's hand and got out of the car. One of the younger wolves from her former pack came at her and she growled low and menacingly. "Let my man go."

"He isn't your man," said Jed, who was the beta of her former pack.

"Oh, but he is. I am mate to the alpha of the New Orleans pack. If you've harmed the pregnant girl inside, you will die. If you withdraw now, I will try to ensure that my mate doesn't hunt you down and kill you for invading his territory and threatening members of his pack." She turned to the one still holding the knife and growled. "I told you to let him go."

"Your true alpha wants you back."

Darby laughed, surprised at the bitterness in the sound. "He is no alpha and his needs or desires no longer concern me."

As the man had still not removed the knife from the driver's throat, Darby whirled and delivered a stunning blow to his head, causing him to stagger and drop the knife. She caught it and grabbed the closest member of the group and now held the knife to his throat. She nodded to the driver. "Get Lily and get her into the car."

"Mistress…"

"Now, Jackson." She watched as he went in and gathered the frightened Lily. "Are you all right?"

Lily nodded. "I will be."

"Go around to the other side of the car and get her inside. Then you get in and drive them out of here."

"I won't leave you, mistress," said Jackson.

"You'll do as I tell you. This group of idiots isn't going to do anything to me. That asshole I was mated to before will want the pleasure of beating me for himself. Get the girls and get out of here." She held his eyes with her own until he nodded in agreement.

He put Lily into the car, got in, and drove off.

"Put the knife down, Darby. We have you outnumbered and we still hold the hostages in the salon. Bobby wants you back," said Jed.

"As I said, what Bobby wants or doesn't want is no longer my concern. But you're right in that you have me outnumbered and have hostages. I'll tell you again, if you leave right now and provided no one's been hurt, I'll persuade Jean-Michel not to hunt you down and kill you. But you'd better start looking for a new alpha. Jean-Michel already wanted Bobby's head on a platter. I doubt now that I'll be able to dissuade him."

"We'll see about that. Bobby plans to challenge his claim to you and your new mate isn't overly popular with the Council." Jed continued to smile at her with his assumed air of authority.

"My mate couldn't give less of a damn about the Council. He holds and protects what's his. As I said, you can leave now and I can assure him that you'll never bother me or ours again. Anything other than that and you won't be breathing by this time next week."

"Put the knife down. You're coming with us."

"Let the people in the salon close up and go home and I will surrender the knife."

Jed indicated that the gang should do as she wanted. She assured the salon manager that everything would be fine and that he should look to his own people's safety. As soon as they had left, Darby let her hostage go, flipped the knife so she had it by the blade, and offered it to Jed.

"Bobby's got plans to knot you the minute he gets hold of you. I'm going to ask him if some of us can watch. And who knows, maybe we'll get a turn."

"Why would you want to watch? He doesn't know what the fuck he's doing with the damn thing and it isn't all that impressive."

Jed slapped her across the face and then grabbed her by the arm and started her back toward their waiting van.

•••••••

Megan watched as they pulled away, leaving Darby to face her former pack alone. "I don't like this. How long will it take our people to mobilize and get into the city? They're at least ninety minutes away, right?"

Gretchen nodded, but Lily said, "No, they're already headed in. The minute those boys stepped into the salon, the hair on the back of my neck stood up. I hit the panic button on my cell phone. They should be close."

"Good thinking, Lily," Gretchen said, turning to Megan. "New Orleans can be a dangerous city. Jean-Michel had panic buttons installed on everyone's cell phones. He's always said he'd much rather respond to a false alarm than not be able to get to someone in time. Do you think they'll hurt her?"

Megan shook her head. "From what little I know, and I never knew it was that bad, Darby's former mate will want to save hurting her for himself." She looked directly at Gretchen. "He'll kill them, won't he?"

"If they put one hair out of place on her head, yes, he will. Either way her former mate is a walking dead man."

"After what I heard today, I can be okay with that. JD said Jean-Michel had been struggling with wanting to honor Darby's wishes in the matter and wanting the man dead by his hand."

Megan was startled when her cell phone buzzed at her. She looked down to see it was JD. "Hey, babe. I've put you on speaker. Everyone is fine, except Darby. They have her. She traded herself for our and the people in the salon's safety."

"But the rest of you are safe? How's Lily?" asked JD.

"I'm fine, JD. Tell Peter to quit worrying. Baby and I are both fine. Worried about Darby, but other than that, fine," said Lily.

JD chuckled. "I'll tell him—won't do any good, but I'll tell him. Jean-Michel wants all of you taken straight home. Geoff and some of the men are there. Once you're inside, the whole place is being put on lockdown until we return. It's her former mate, isn't it?"

"Not him personally, but his people. JD, I'm afraid of what he'll do to her. She's not the same mate who ran from him in terror. You should have seen her take the knife away from one guy and then use it to hold another one hostage until we could get away. She was incredible."

"No wonder the old bastards at the Council were afraid of Bae Diogel," said Gretchen.

"As long as the rest of you are safe, we'll deal with these bastards. Jean-Michel has already put the Council on notice that they invaded our territory, threatened our women, and took his mate as hostage. He intends to show them no mercy. Be safe. We'll be home with Darby just as soon as we can be."

•••••••

JD hung up at the phone and looked at his lifelong friend. "You heard?"

"Yes. I want to be angry that she exchanged her safety for others. But I can't. She did what needed doing. I am humbled to be mated to such a woman."

"As well you should be."

"Let's go teach these bastards a lesson about invading our city and daring to threaten our mates."

It was all JD could do to refrain from recoiling from the

malicious look in the eyes of his friend. That Darby's former mate would die was no longer a question. Whether Jean-Michel would wipe out the entire male side of that pack would depend on whether or not they had harmed Darby.

They sped into the city ready to retake what had been stolen from them. Jean-Michel had been able to locate the private airport and plane that the pack planned to use to spirit Darby away. If they failed to stop them within the city, stopping that plane would become paramount. He knew the men he had dispatched would not fail him.

•••••••

Darby sat quietly wedged between two of her former pack members, one she remembered as being fairly sympathetic. He leaned over to her. "You shouldn't have run from him. Bobby was all kinds of upset. Then when you and those bitches at Bae Diogel messed him up, he was really pissed. But mating with this guy… you'd better hope he didn't get you knocked up. Bobby won't stand for you to whelp another wolf's cub."

"You know, Jimmy, I always thought for one of his apes you were a fairly decent guy. But what Bobby wants, thinks, or does isn't going to be a problem for much longer. My mate will kill him. I'm now debating the wisdom of not taking Jean-Michel up on his offer the night he ran me to ground to have Bobby's head delivered to me on a platter. You and this group of idiots would only help yourself by dropping me off at a nice restaurant where I can get a cocktail and call my mate to come pick me up. I may be able to persuade him to let the lot of you live… but that isn't a given."

"Shut your hole, woman," said Jed from the front seat. "Bobby's gonna teach you good."

Darby eyed him with quiet self-confidence. "Bobby won't live to see the end of the week. And your chances aren't looking too good either, Jed. If my mate learns you're one of the men who raped me, he'll rip your throat out with his bare hands."

"It isn't rape when your alpha tells you that you can use his woman's pussy for your enjoyment. And you were always such a hot piece of tail. I looked forward to it when Bobby had too much to drink. I always made sure I was sober so that I could have a turn with you. Only wish he'd let me put my seed in you instead of all over your back. I'll bet I could have put a baby in your belly."

She smiled. "Doubtful. You know I'm going to enjoy watching you die. Maybe Jean-Michel will let me do it myself."

"You wait until we get on that plane. I'm gonna call Bobby and see if he won't let me take my belt to you as beta of our pack. That'll give you something to think about on the way home."

"My home is in the opposite direction. But he's coming for you, Jed. You might want to use what little time you have left to say your goodbyes to anyone who gives a damn."

"Geesh, Darby, don't egg him on. You want him to use you rough again?" said Jimmy.

The phone rang; Jed smiled. "Now we'll see what's what, missy." He hit the speaker function. "We got her, Bobby. And she's a lot sassier than I remembered. You want me to give her a good whipping before we get home? She could sure use it."

"Nah. I'm going to tan her hide when she gets here and then I'll give her a good knotting. I got one really starting to bulge. It's gonna feel good shoving it up her cunt four or five times before shooting my load in her."

Darby shook her head but showed no fear. "You do know, you illiterate goon, that you haven't a clue as to how to properly knot and tie a woman."

"I don't know, you screamed pretty good each time I did you."

"Yeah, but what's supposed to happen is that you mount your mate, force the knot, and then seal her to you. That way when you flood her, your cum stays inside her. Then you're tied together for a couple of hours. It's truly an amazing experience. Jean-Michel knotted me several times already at my request. And by the way? I no longer carry your mark. He got rid of that and I now proudly carry his."

"You bitch! Who do you think you are, talking to me that way?"

"I know exactly who I am. I am the mate to Jean-Michel Gautier, the alpha of New Orleans. And, by the way, the man who's going to end your and Jed's lives."

Darby had been keeping a close eye on the men in the van. Most of them had become increasingly uncomfortable with the conversation. She wished she believed it was because they were seeing how she had been wronged. She suspected, however, the idea that their deaths might be imminent was more the source of their discomfort.

After a few more minutes and numerous insults, Darby ceased to engage with Bobby or Jed. Jed hung up the phone, chuckling. "Just you wait, missy, he's gonna beat your ass and fuck your cunt raw. He'll learn you this time. He may just keep you naked and chained to the bed."

"You know, boys. It's only Jed here who harmed me. I'm pretty sure my mate would let you go with your lives if you overpower him and keep me safe. If you follow this asshole and that lunatic he's beta for, you're going to end up dead."

"You boys quit listening to that gal. We're gonna be just fine. We get her home and we can start looking for some gals for you. Hell, I'm gonna tell Bobby we ought to get some professional girls out to service you boys."

Darby shook her head. "Never going to happen. You'll all be dead by then." She turned to Jimmy. "So, tell me, are the only women still Maryann and Heather?"

"Yeah, we haven't been able to find mates for the rest of us. Bobby's talking about doing a raid and turning some humans."

"You boys really are too stupid to live," she said.

"Why'd you want to know about the gals back home?"

"I want to ask Jean-Michel if he'd be willing to offer them his protection until they can decide what they want to do."

"What do you mean? Heather's mate is back home and Maryann's is here with us," said Jimmy, who was beginning to understand that the woman who had fled in terror from Bobby had been replaced by a strong, confident woman who had apparently mated with a powerful alpha.

Darby turned and looked him directly in the eye. "I'm telling you, they're all going to be dead. Jean-Michel will wipe your bloody awful pack off the face of this earth. And I'm going to ask if I can help." She turned away from him and looked straight out the window.

The van continued on in silence.

CHAPTER FIFTEEN

The SUV containing the bulk of Jean-Michel's men were now in route to the private airport. The men at the airport had reported that the plane was being readied for takeoff. Jean-Michel's instructions were to contain the men who had Darby and to avoid killing them if at all possible. But regardless, that plane was not to leave and Darby's safety was to be their primary concern.

•••••••

The van pulled into the private airport. Darby kept expecting to feel afraid or concerned, but she wasn't. She knew Jean-Michel and her pack were coming for her. She had yet to be able to sense his presence, but she knew it wouldn't be long. She knew she would fight them tooth and nail before she got on that plane.

They pulled out on the tarmac and rolled up to the plane. There didn't seem to be anyone moving around, but none of the idiots in the van seemed to notice. Darby forced herself to stay relaxed but vigilant. The van came to a stop and the doors were opened. She was taken out of the van and they started toward the plane.

As they got closer to the stairway into the plane, Darby waited for fear or panic to overtake her. It didn't. Instead what she felt was Jean-Michel's soothing presence. He was here; he had come for her. She never doubted that he would, but it felt good nonetheless to feel him so close.

Jed bounded up the steps into the plane, only to come flying back out and tumbling down them, followed by men Darby recognized as belonging to her pack. It had been Jake who had punched Jed in the face. Darby knew because he was rubbing his fist. The men surrounding her reached for concealed weapons.

"Not a good idea, boys. Jean-Michel would prefer you not be harmed. But he's a very flexible kind of guy. As long as Darby isn't hurt, you may yet live to see the end of the day." He spotted the red mark on her face from Jed's earlier slap. "Darby? Are you all right, mistress?"

She touched her cheek. "This? I'm fine. I think you did far more damage to Jed's face than he did to mine."

Two of her pack mates descended the stairs and grabbed Jed before he could do anything. The other men who had been holding her let go of her arms and tried to become very small. The anger and violence bubbling beneath the surface was palpable. Darby approached Jed and smiled.

"Your life isn't worth spit," said Darby as she spat in his face.

"Mistress," Jake said, "please get away from him. Jean-Michel won't want you standing in the middle of all of this."

"Jake, what have I told you about formal titles. If you're are going to refer to my mate as Jean-Michel, you'd best start referring to me as Darby." She walked calmly away from the men who had been holding her captive. She heard the other SUV pull up and saw her mate exit the vehicle.

"Darby, beloved, are you all right?" he said, joining her. The red mark on her face did not go unnoticed. He touched it gently and turned to Jake. "Who?"

"The one with the broken nose and Darby's spit on him. She just informed him his life was not worth spit."

"She would be correct." He kissed her gently. "Did any of the rest of them harm you in any way?"

"No, Jean-Michel. I'm fine. The other girls are all fine, right? Jackson got them to safety?"

"Yes. He was very upset that you sent him away. I assured him he did the right thing."

"I'm surprised you got here so fast."

"Lily hit her cell phone's panic button the minute these bastards entered the nail salon. Forgive me for not ensuring both your and Megan's phones had the application installed. It will be done as soon as we get home."

Darby watched Jed as the realization hit him that by striking her, he had sealed his own death warrant. She smiled and kissed Jean-Michel. "I'd like to speak to you about what you're planning to do in response to this attack on our pack."

"That one," Jean-Michel said, pointing to Jed, "and the bastard whose mark I removed from your body will die. I will not allow them to live."

"I sort of figured that. But the rest of these idiots are just that—idiots who haven't a clue as to who they were following or why."

"You think I should let them go?"

"Not exactly. I'm thinking we take their plane back and raid the farm. There are two women there who, like me, were brought in against their will. One is wolf-born, the other human, who was turned without her consent. I would ask you to offer them your protection until they can figure out what they want to do."

"And?"

"I was hoping after you killed Bobby, because I'm pretty sure he's a dead man walking," Jean-Michel nodded, "that you'd burn that farm to the ground and let the rest shift for themselves. It won't be easy for any of them to find a pack that would have them. And life is not very nice to lone wolves."

"Again, my mate, you show such great courage and

heart. How am I to deny you what you ask?"

"I'm sure you could find a way. I just think you're still riding on the buzz from the number of times you knotted me in the past few days." She grinned at him before kissing him again.

He chuckled. "You are a most naughty mate. Perhaps I need to take you home and knot you again to remind you who is your alpha."

She wound her arms around him. "I have no need for a reminder as I am quite clear about to whom it is that I am mated. However, I wouldn't mind spending a significant amount of time in our bed tied to you."

"Darby, you can't just let him kill me," pleaded Jed.

Before the words had barely left his mouth, JD had produced a scimitar dagger and cut the man's throat.

"He was mine to kill," growled Jean-Michel.

"No, the bastard who was Darby's mate is yours. This was his beta and was mine. You forget your mate offered her safety to ensure the safety of my mate."

Jean-Michel thought for a moment. "I can see the reasoning behind that. We'll need to dispose of the body."

"We can fly out over the ocean and just drop him into it. That's what we did with the Serbs—only we weighted them down and took them out on the boat," said Darby in a cheerful and helpful tone.

Jean-Michel laughed. "My mate is so helpful, *n'est pas*?"

His men joined in his laughter and watched as the men who had been holding Darby began to pee on themselves and plead for their lives.

Jean-Michel watched them with disgust. "These men are pathetic. Are you sure you don't want them disposed of in the same way?"

"No, they aren't worth the trouble. Just wipe out their farm so that they have nothing. I'll bet I can transfer all the money from the account to you. Then you could use that as a dowry of sorts for Maryann and Heather. We should drag them back with us to the farm. After you kill Bobby, although I think I have the better claim on both his life and Jed's, they can watch you torch the place and leave with the girls. Maybe we could have our plane pick us up?"

Peter, Lily's mate, chimed in. "She has an excellent plan, Jean-Michel. And who knows, maybe given some time to recover from what must have been a horrible ordeal, one or both of these girls will find someone within our own ranks."

JD looked to their alpha. "He makes a good point, Jean-Michel. Other than a better claim to kill their alpha—which by the way, Darby, is complete bullshit—I think your mate has an excellent plan."

"Peter, why don't you take Darby back to the plantation and see to your mate. I don't want the stress of this afternoon to jeopardize her pregnancy."

Darby interrupted him. "Jean-Michel, no. I need to go. Heather and Maryann will never come with you willingly unless I'm there."

"In case it's missed your notice, I have become quite adept at bringing home little girls who don't want to be brought."

"Please, Jean-Michel. It would make it easier for them. If I subordinate my claim to yours to kill Bobby?"

"And you admit that you should have allowed me to kill him to begin with."

She smiled. "Yes, Jean-Michel."

JD snorted and the rest of the pack grinned. "I'm not quite sure which of you has the other wrapped around his or her little finger."

•••••••

After they bound and gagged the remaining members of Darby's former pack, the plane took off and headed out over open water; it dipped below radar and Jed's body, which had been weighted down, was tossed out the door. Watching the men who had once called him beta watch as his body was so casually disposed of gave Darby great satisfaction. They were now terrorized and she might have felt sorry for them except for the fact that she had spent several years in their company beaten and terrorized on a daily basis.

The plane landed on a long-abandoned airstrip. The pilot of the plane was himself a lone wolf and had informed Jean-Michel that should his services ever be needed, the New Orleans pack could count on him and his discretion.

Darby was happy to see Jackson get off the plane. Jean-Michel explained to her that he served as both driver and pilot. He greeted her warmly and brought the good wishes of the rest of the pack to her.

Jean-Michel dispersed his men and quickly had the farmhouse surrounded and the two women separated from the males of the pack. The women were brought out first. Both were overjoyed to see Darby and ran to embrace her.

"Bobby said he was bringing you back," whispered Heather. "He is furious with you for leaving, for the beat-down you gave him a couple of years back and for now being with this pack."

Darby smiled. "Bobby is, as ever, full of shit. Heather and Maryann, allow me the pleasure of introducing you to my mate, Jean-Michel Gautier, alpha of the New Orleans pack. My beloved, this is Heather and Maryann, the only bright spots in the darkness that was my existence here. I can't tell you the number of times they nursed me back from the brink of death even though I didn't want them to."

Jean-Michel kissed each of their hands, noting to himself how rough and callused they were from hard work—much more than those of the men of this place. "If my Darby is here because of you then I owe you a debt I can never repay."

The men were brought out and forced to their knees. Darby took Bobby's cell phone and called the local bank arranging for the money to be transferred immediately to the plantation's account.

"You can't just come in here, steal my woman and all my

money. I'm going to take you before the Council," said Bobby as he got to his feet.

His one show of bravado quickly faded when Jean-Michel turned to look at him, his eyes blazing.

"You will take no one any place. Before the sun sets, you will be dead. You will die knowing that my mate was never yours. You may have possessed and abused her body, but she never belonged to you. You never knew the sweetness of her surrender or the heat of her passion. I have already informed the Council that by invading my city and kidnapping my mate that I would see you dead. I invited the Council to try to raise those packs that they could to try to stop me… they declined my invitation. You have a choice; I can kill you where you stand or you can challenge me to combat in either wolf or human form. If you choose the former, which I really hope you don't, I will end your miserable existence quickly and relatively painlessly. Choose to fight and I will enjoy tearing you limb from limb and offering your entrails to my mate to burn."

"Wait. Darby, you can't let him kill me."

"Oh, I didn't want to, Bobby, but he didn't want me to mess up my fifty-dollar manicure to do it myself." She glanced down nonchalantly at her nails. "Damn, one of my nails has smudged."

"Do not fret, beloved," Jean-Michel said as he nuzzled her neck and wrapped his arm around her waist. "I'll get you another manicure." He turned back toward Bobby, whose face had lost all of its coloring. "Choose."

"Jean-Michel?"

"Yes, my beloved?"

"Could you just kill him and be done with it. I'd like to get Maryann and Heather back to the plantation and I'm starving. I can't wait to see what Claudine has prepared for supper."

"Would that please you to see him die quickly?"

"I don't particularly care how he dies as long as he's dead. But I am hungry and I'd like to get the girls home and settled."

"As you wish." In the blink of an eye, Jean-Michel produced a scimitar dagger and neatly severed Bobby's jugular vein. He was dead before he hit the ground. "Put the body in the farmhouse and set this place on fire. Cut the others loose and let's get the ladies back to the plane." Jean-Michel turned to the women. "Is there anything you wish to take with you? You will be provided with all that you need once we are home."

Both women shook their heads. Before Darby could reach out to them, JD and Peter introduced themselves, took them by the hand, and led them toward the plane. Heather, who was being led away by JD, looked back at Darby.

Darby smiled. "He's fine, Heather. JD is our beta and mated to one of my friends from Bae Diogel. He's a good man, although I'd prefer if you kept my opinion of him to yourself." Heather giggled as Darby had intended her to do. "Sweetheart, before we leave, can you get each of those two bastards to sign some sort of release so we don't have to jump through all kinds of hoops to get their pairings dissolved?"

"It would be easier to kill them."

"Yes, I know, but messier. You'd be happy to sign, wouldn't you, boys?"

Both men nodded vehemently. Jean-Michel put something down on paper and had each man sign in his own blood. The house and out buildings were torched and the men cut loose. Jean-Michel led his people back to the plane.

Darby giggled. "Signing in blood? That was a bit much, don't you think?"

Jean-Michel smiled. "Perhaps, but when those men speak of what happened here today, others may think twice before attacking us or treating their women badly. Before you even ask, I will not see them rushed into anything. I think they have suffered almost as much as you. We will let them heal. They will have our protection and no one, unless called to them as a fated mate, will have them without their wholehearted consent."

"You do know I adore you, don't you?"

"You've mentioned it a time or two but usually when tied to me or at the height of our passion. My fragile male ego may have to hear it more often than that."

She laughed out loud. "There is nothing fragile about your ego, but I will endeavor to tell you so often you get sick of hearing it."

"That, my beloved, would never happen."

He wrapped his arm around her and headed for the plane to take them home.

CHAPTER SIXTEEN

The pack had once again gathered in the main house to greet those who had gone to deal with Darby's former mate. Darby was hugged repeatedly and praised for her bravery in trading her safety to ensure the others were protected.

Darby scanned the room and saw Summer was among them. Summer crossed over to her and hugged her close.

"Darby, thank God, you're safe. I've been so worried."

"You have?" Darby said, eyeing her with suspicion.

Summer had the good grace to blush. "Yes. I heard what had happened. I knew Geoff was worried. So was I. I couldn't bear the thought of something happening to you and that the last words we'd ever spoken were done in anger and recrimination. I got pretty upset… with myself."

"It's been a difficult time, Summer. For all of us. It's been hard for the rest of us to embrace the happiness we've found knowing you were so miserable. But you wouldn't even give yourself a chance while we were at Calon Gwyllt."

"Probably because my mate wasn't there," she said sheepishly.

Darby couldn't mask the look of shock on her face. "You don't say…"

"I heard what had happened and asked to speak to

Geoff. I didn't want to be upstairs while all of the men were so upset. I told him I'd give him my word not to try anything until Jean-Michel initiated the run. The men Jean-Michel left behind were none too happy about being left. Geoff worked his butt off to keep them from just kind of losing it. And most of the ones here weren't even the mates of the women with you. I tried to see what I could do to help everybody. It felt good to be part of this pack. Felt like we were back at Bae Diogel… only with testosterone."

Darby giggled. "It is different. And it is male-dominated but these are truly good men. But let's skip the bullshit. What did you mean about your mate not being at Calon Gwyllt?"

"You know exactly what I mean."

Darby giggled again. "Yes, I do. Annoying, isn't it?"

Summer laughed out loud. "Very."

"So, you're not going to run?"

"No, I think I've caused enough drama, don't you?"

"Probably. But you'll probably cause more. We Bae Diogel girls tend to be a bit on the melodramatic side."

Megan joined them, hugging Darby. "If you ever pull a stunt like that again, don't you dare leave me behind or send me off with others. And what's Summer not going to be overly dramatic about?"

Summer grinned at her. Megan started laughing.

Still smiling, Megan continued, "Oh, my God, you mean you've actually pulled your head out of your ass long enough to see Geoff is terrific and your fated mate?"

"Apparently I'm not as quick to figure these things out as you and Darby."

"So, have you formally accepted his claim?"

Summer shook her head.

"Do you want to put the poor guy out of his misery and do so in front of Jean-Michel and JD? I'm sure I can get them to excuse themselves long enough to let you do so."

"No, I think since I've had the whole pack in an uproar, they ought to get to see me admit what was obvious to the rest of you." Summer left them to join Geoff and put her arm around him, which he reciprocated as though he'd been doing so for a long, long time.

JD and Jean-Michel looked at each other and then turned toward their mates, whose bright smiles and nodding heads answered their unasked question. The two women joined their mates. Before Jean-Michel could address his pack, Megan leaned over to him and whispered, "Had them sign it in blood? And your mate says we're the dramatic ones."

Jean-Michel laughed, called for the attention of the pack, and asked Vachon to gather the household staff. Once everyone was assembled, he introduced the newest members of the pack, Maryann and Heather. He was delighted to see they were far more relaxed now than they had been. It would seem even without an introduction, his pack and staff had made them feel welcome.

He then led his pack in a round of applause for Darby's bravery in protecting the women and the nail salon employees. He advised Vachon to send them a really large tip for their inconvenience. He also lauded Darby's generosity not only in extending pack status to Heather and Maryann, but in allowing all but the alpha and beta of her former pack to live.

"And last, but certainly not least… when last we were gathered together—was it only this morning?"

Laughter rumbled through the group.

Jean-Michel smiled. "Summer had rejected Geoff's claim on her as a mate and had opted to run. I understand that there has been a change in plans and a change of heart."

Summer released her hold on Geoff and approached Jean-Michel. She took his hands in hers and brought them up to her face where she rubbed first her forehead and then her cheeks along them before kissing them. "Jean-Michel Gautier, I ask that you accept me into your pack so that I may call you alpha and be given your protection."

He smiled at her. "It was always yours, Summer.

Welcome home."

She smiled at him and turned to look at Geoff, who had tears in his eyes and a grin that spread from ear to ear.

He crossed, taking her hands in his. "Summer, I claim you as my mate in this lifetime and all the ones that follow. Do you accept my claim?"

She threw her arms around his neck and pressed her body into his. "I do. You know I do. I can't think of anything I'd rather do."

Jean-Michel laughed and clapped his hands together. "Now that we have that settled, Claudine assures me she has enough food prepared to feed a gathering twice our size. I assured her that we had more than the appetite for everything to do it justice."

Everyone started into the huge dining hall and began helping themselves. Darby started to worry about Heather and Maryann, but saw that Summer was already stepping into her role as mate to the omega of the pack. This was the Summer she had known at Bae Diogel—kind, funny, and loving.

The pack laughed and enjoyed each other's company until late into the night. Jean-Michel was just about to spirit Darby up to their bed when Vachon beckoned. There was a note from the Council and one from Dylan Grainger of Calon Gwyllt. He asked Vachon to quietly get JD and Geoff to the library; their mates were welcome but not mandatory.

The six of them gathered in the library. Jean-Michel smiled at Summer. "I'm glad you have decided to embrace your fate with us. Geoff may well need a strong, determined mate to help see us through what's coming."

"Is it bad? Is it something we caused either as Bae Diogel or today?" asked Darby.

"Dylan and I talked about this briefly before we left Calon Gwyllt. Neither Bae Diogel nor what happened today is what caused what's coming, but it certainly added fuel to the fire. There are those at the Ruling Council who wish to see some of the stronger packs brought to heel and follow the old ways. We, and there are more than a few of us, aren't willing to walk backwards into history. We must embrace the new. They refuse to see that the European packs are gearing up for something. They want to believe it's just more of the same old saber rattling. But the raid on Bae Diogel was pretty extreme—not only did one pack attack another, but it was a European pack against a North American pack and the Europeans did nothing. They haven't so much as imposed a single sanction on the Serbs. The Serbs and their ilk are gaining power all over Europe. The Ruling Council would have us bury our heads in the sand. In my opinion, and the opinion of those whom I respect, all that will get us is kicked in the ass. Dylan is calling for a meeting of the packs that stood with us in voting against the action taken against Bae Diogel and the Charleston and Savannah packs, both of whom chose neutrality."

JD said, "A kind of war council?"

"Hopefully we can avoid that, but if it comes to it, yes. Dylan suggested we hold it here. New Orleans is easy to slip in and out of and the plantation is big enough to hold everyone. Dylan said he would understand if we chose to play a less aggressive role in what's coming. He knows that we're about to get a reprimand from the Council…"

"We've had those before," said Geoff. All three women looked at him. "Let's just say anyone studying history shouldn't be surprised that three of you from Bae Diogel ended up here with the only wolf who is a direct and legitimate descendant of a pirate."

Jean-Michel chuckled. "He mentioned that he has contacted Oliver up in the Hamptons as well as the packs in Charleston and Savannah. I think alphas and their mates. We could be talking about twenty adults. I'm not sure how many have children. Darby, you'll need to coordinate with Vachon, Mrs. Hastings, and Claudine to get geared up for this. And it's a small window. We need to get this done within the month."

He turned to Geoff. "I'm afraid, my friend, that all we can allow you with your Summer is a very brief honeymoon. And as soon as Lily is safely delivered, we need Peter to set up a network around the country and Canada... Europe if he can manage it. The more intel we have the better."

"If you're looking for electronics, there's nobody better than Anna at Calon Gwyllt. Maybe Dylan should bring her and her mate Josh with them so she and Peter can coordinate," offered Darby.

They all agreed it was an excellent idea. "We should go make a brief appearance back out at the party. Make sure Maryann and Heather are settled," said Jean-Michel.

"That's been seen to, Jean-Michel," said Summer, to everyone's surprise. "I didn't figure this was a let's shoot tequila in celebration of Summer, as Megan so aptly put it, getting her head out of her ass type gathering. I asked Gretchen to kind of look after them and she said she'd be happy to do it. But if they haven't already retired for the evening, I'll make sure they're okay. I think Darby and Megan have done enough for one day."

They left the library and started rounding people up to close the gathering for the evening. Claudine promised a sumptuous repast for the morning.

Darby said, smiling, "Dear Claudine, do you know how to prepare anything different?" and everyone agreed. The pack started dispersing and both Heather and Maryann made sure to thank Darby for thinking of them and coming to get them and Jean-Michel for offering them his protection.

Darby and Jean-Michel were the last ones to climb the stairs. They opened the doors to their suite and saw that the bed had been turned back and the curtains drawn. "Mrs. Hastings never misses a beat, does she?"

"I assure you, beloved, this is all you. She never once turned back my bed for me."

Darby walked out onto the balcony and watched the river as the moon reflected down onto it. She'd come to love the Mississippi in the very short time she'd been here. It had moods—it could be fast flowing and stormy or it could be like tonight, just lazing along its way or anything and everything in between.

"What troubles you?" he asked softly. "And do not lie to me and tell me nothing." He ran his hand down her flank. "I would prefer not to knot and tie you on a sore bottom."

"You know me too well already. I just worry that something will happen to our pack… to this place."

"This pack and this plantation have stood more than three hundred years. One of the things passed down through our line was to never be caught unaware or unprepared. We've been stockpiling things for the past five years. Jean Lafitte had a great network of hiding places and we are using all of them. Whatever comes, we will prevail. We always have, and this time we will not be standing in the darkness by ourselves. It is time the stronger, more progressive packs left the shadows and forced all of the packs to embrace the light."

She smiled at him, loving him more than she ever thought it would be possible. "For the record," she said, drawing her finger down his core, "I am not tied to you nor are we at the height of our passion. I love and adore you. You have done nothing but bring joy and rapture to my life. I pledge to love you for the rest of this life and all the lives to come."

"Then come to bed, mate. Let me show you again what else the Gautier alphas are known for…"

Jean-Michel led her back to their bed and did just that.

THE END

STORMY NIGHT PUBLICATIONS WOULD LIKE TO THANK YOU FOR YOUR INTEREST IN OUR BOOKS.

If you liked this book (or even if you didn't), we would really appreciate you leaving a review on the site where you purchased it. Reviews provide useful feedback for us and for our authors, and this feedback (both positive comments and constructive criticism) allows us to work even harder to make sure we provide the content our customers want to read.

If you would like to check out more books from Stormy Night Publications, if you want to learn more about our company, or if you would like to join our mailing list, please visit our website at:

www.stormynightpublications.com

Manufactured by Amazon.ca
Acheson, AB